James York

Count Lucanor

Or, the fifty pleasant stories of Patronio

James York

Count Lucanor
Or, the fifty pleasant stories of Patronio

ISBN/EAN: 9783744750493

Printed in Europe, USA, Canada, Australia, Japan

Cover: Foto ©Andreas Hilbeck / pixelio.de

More available books at **www.hansebooks.com**

COUNT LUCANOR; OR THE

Fifty Pleasant Stories

Of Patronio

WRITTEN BY THE PRINCE DON JUAN MANUEL

AND FIRST DONE INTO ENGLISH BY

JAMES YORK, M.D., 1868

GIBBINGS & COMPANY, LIMITED

18 BURY STREET, LONDON, W.C.

1899

PREFACE.

IN introducing for the first time in England one of the choicest productions of early Spanish literature—a book written a century before the invention of printing—it may be as well to say a few words as to the author and the times in which he lived.

Don Juan Manuel was born in Escalona, on the 5th May, 1282. His father, Don Pedro Manuel, a brother of Alfonso the Wise, died when he was two years old. Don Juan was educated by his cousin, Sancho IV, and lived with him on the same familiar terms as his father had with Alfonso. He exhibited early those warlike tendencies which characterized all the great Spanish nobles of that time; in 1294, while yet a boy, he was already in the field against the Moors.

Under Ferdinand IV, who succeeded Sancho, and knew how to appreciate the qualities of Don Manuel, the latter reached, at the age of twenty-eight, to the highest employments of the State. Unfortunately, Ferdinand, dying in 1312, left his successor, Alfonso XI, only thirteen months old, which gave rise to

rent of Portugal; much, however, against the wish
of Alphonso, who was touched, perhaps, with a
too tardy regret for his breach of faith, or with a
jealous aversion that another should supersede him
in the affections of her whom he had so grossly
outraged. Meanwhile, Don Manuel, after waging
victorious war for the king against the Moors, died,
at the age of sixty-five, in 1347.

Allied by descent and marriage with nearly all
the royal families of Spain and Portugal, Don Juan
Manuel may be considered as a type of those ancient
Spanish nobles, whose pride of lineage, whose fierce
courage, and chivalrous sentiment are traditional.
These characteristics, however, he shared with many
others of his time, and they would hardly have
served to make his name remembered. The distinguishing and exceptional fact that causes it to
stand out conspicuous from the rest, is his author-
ship. His victories and defeats, his royal relationship and descent are nothing to us now; while the
very thing upon which he probably prided himself
least, or looked upon as at best an idle solace from
graver toils—the collection of stories which he
penned in the rare intervals of leisure between the
labours of the camp and the council, and which he
bequeathed in manuscript to the monks of Peñafiel—
still lives to be read, and to afford instruction and
entertainment to a generation that follows the arts
of peace as nobler than the arts of war

El Conde Lucano? first found its way into print in 1575, when it was published at Seville, under the auspices of Argote de Molina, whose elaborate genealogy of the author would delight a heraldic mind. It was again printed, at Madrid, in 1642,* after which time, in the general neglect all over Europe of early literature, it lay forgotten for nearly two centuries.

An incomplete edition, with modernized spelling, was published at Stuttgart in 1839, and reprinted at Paris in 1840. An edition was also published at Barcelona in 1853. But the first critical edition presenting a standard text, founded on an elaborate collation of the earlier editions and of the existing manuscripts, appeared only seven years ago (Madrid, 1860), under the superintendence of Don Pascual de Gayangos. In this edition the missing chapter, the absence of which renders the two early ones incomplete, was supplied from a manuscript in the National Library at Madrid.

It is indeed time that such a book, so full of the antique simplicity and wisdom, should be appreciated. The artless *naïveté* of these tales ought to delight an age surfeited with the sensational novels that pour from our circulating libraries in an uninterrupted stream. Of analysis of character,

---

* The editions of 1575 and 1642 are among the rarest books in the world

indeed, about which so much cry is made now-a-days, there is little. It was an age when men were not always probing their moral sensations and analysing their own minds with a morbid self-consciousness. It was a robust, healthy age, little given to fret itself with metaphysical or fine-spun distinctions; an age of muscular activity, not over prone to much speculation, and what there was of abstract thought was so clear and transparent that he who runs may read.

And so, though every tale in the collection illustrates some wise moral and closes with some pithy maxim for the conduct of life, there is no dogmatic teaching. Every reader could apply the tale in his own way, and adapt the moral to the peculiar circumstances of his own condition. And, independently of any moral, each story is a real story, artistic and interesting—nay, *true* in the best sense of the word, true to nature and the human heart.

The book is further a picture of the time. Any one who wishes to have a living representation of the Spanish chivalry of the fourteenth century, of the life and manners of that picturesque epoch, of the blunt nobleness and rude valour of which the Cid is still cherished in Spain as a type—will find it here, if anywhere.

What shall we say as to the *literary* merit of the book? Written more than a century before the invention of printing, long before modern writing became a practice and an art—at a time when the few scholars who wrote used Latin as the only fitting and permanent vehicle of their thoughts—it has, doubtless, what we at this day may call faults of style, with occasional needless and somewhat wearisome repetitions ; these the translator found it difficult to abridge without interfering with the characteristic features of the original, as regards quaintness and clearness of detail—two qualities which constitute the charm of the book, and are essential to the force and point of able literature.

Like our Chaucer, Don Juan Manuel has a high claim to the reverence of his countrymen as one of the first who consolidated their language, and discarding 'canine-latin' (Ciceronian having become impossible), gave to the Castilian dialect a permanence and importance, at the same time improving and enlarging its capabilities of expression.

From the Arabic phrases which we find scattered through the book, it may safely be assumed that Don Manuel had, during his long intercourse with the Moors, become tolerably proficient in that language. This inference lends probability to the idea that some of the Eastern collections of tales were not unknown to him, and that he may have drawn considerably from such sources in some of his narratives.

Considering the general character of the literature of those times, "Count Lucanor" is singularly free from grossness. There is not, indeed, one instance of intentional impurity in the whole book ; so that it may safely be placed in the hands of children with-

out fear of contamination.   If there be any likeness
to the Decameron, it is rather in the mediæval
abandon and simplicity of both the narrators than
in their subjects ; for there is, as we say, no trace
in Don Manuel of the licentiousness of his more
famous Italian contemporary.

It has been the translator's aim to preserve, as
much as possible, all the characteristic features of
the original.   While avoiding archaic words, which
would render the book distasteful and difficult to the
general reader, he has purposely chosen a somewhat
antique style, to correspond as far as might be with
his author's.   The most laborious, and, perhaps, the
least satisfactory portion of his task has been his
endeavour to render the couplets which wind up the
tales by corresponding English couplets, without
departing too widely from the original, or adhering
to it so closely as to be stilted.

The notes appended to each chapter consist prin-
cipally of historical and literary illustrations necessary
to the complete understanding of the tales themselves,
which, from their antiquity, may easily be supposed
to contain many allusions to events and to persons
now grown somewhat obscure.   In some of these
the translator has been considerably indebted to the
researches of M. Adolphe de Puibusque, whose
French version of "Count Lucanor" was published
in 1854.*

---

* There exists also a German translation by Eichendorff. We
are not aware that the book has appeared in any other language.

The advantages of fabular or allegorical teaching are too well understood to need any comment. Don Manuel, however, enjoys the distinction of being free from the cynicism and covert sarcasm which mar the instructiveness of too many writers of this class. He has been able to paint vice and folly in their true colours, without degrading human nature to point a clever epigram. For that satire only is wise and good which has in it an undercurrent of tenderness and pity for those foibles which the satirist himself shares, more or less, with his fellow-men.

We trust that "Count Lucanor" may be accepted by the English reader as a genuine, if rugged piece of ore from that rich mine of early Spanish literature which yet lies hidden and unwrought.

London, 1868.

CONTENTS.

THE PROLOGUE.

AMONGST the many strange things that our Lord God made, He thought good to make one very marvellous. That is, that of the numberless men who are in the world, there is not one who altogether resembles another in face. All men's features, indeed, are made up of the same parts, but these parts are not the same in one as in another. And since in the features, which take up so small a place, there is to be found so great a variety, it is less to be wondered at that there should be a difference in the mind and will of men, and that you should find no man in these respects altogether like another. And I will give you a few examples that you may the better understand this.

Men, who seek and desire to serve God, all seek one thing, but they do not all serve Him in the same manner; for some serve Him in one way, others in another. Or again, those who serve their lords, all serve them, but all do not serve them in one and the same manner.

Again, those who labour in the fields, or rear stock,
or manufacture, or hunt, have all different methods
of doing the same thing. From these and many
other examples, too long to relate, you will understand that, although all men possess will, mind, and
feelings alike, little as they resemble each other in
features, still less do they in these other qualities:
and each acquires a greater fitness and aptitude,
where self-interest is the stimulant; so, if you wish
to convey your knowledge to another, endeavour to
convince him that it is for his own interest. And
as many men do not understand subtle or abstract
matters, hence it is that they derive no pleasure from
books, or writings, which treat only of such subjects;
and consequently can never appreciate or understand
them. And therefore I, Don Juan, son of the Infant Don Manuel, Governor of the frontiers and
kingdom of Murcia, composed this book, using
therein the choicest expressions I could find; introducing also many examples which may benefit
those who hear them; and this I did following the
example of the physicians who, in their treatment of
the liver, mix with their medicines sugar, honey, or
something to make them more agreeable.* So is it
when any other member of the body is affected,

---

* Compare Tasso, Ger. Lib. 1. 3.

    " So we, if children young diseased we find,
       Anoint with sweets the vessel's foremost parts,
    To make them taste the potions sharp we give;
    They drink deceived; and so deceived they live."
                    FAIRFAX's *translation.*

each requires its own proper remedy; and this rule I will, with the blessing of God, adopt in this book, so that all who read it may be benefited and amused at the same time, and they shall not have the excuse to say that, being tiresome and dry, the good advice therein was lost; for, like the palatable ingredients combined with the bitter medicines essential for the complaint, so the beauty and aptness of the language which I have endeavoured to convey in this book shall render the moral inseparable from the story.

And God, who is the author and giver of all good, will I trust, in His mercy, cause all who read this book to derive benefit therefrom both in soul and body; knowing this to be my desire and intention in writing it; and He will attribute any faults committed therein to the weakness of my understanding, and not to perverseness of spirit. And if any good be derived therefrom, I and my readers should thank God for it, He being the author and source of all light and truth. And now we will commence the book in the manner of a dialogue between Count Lucanor and his friendly adviser Patronio.

COUNT LUCANOR.

CHAPTER I.

*Relates to what happened to a Moorish king
of Cordova.*

NE day Count Lucanor spoke to Patronio
his friend after this manner :—

"Patronio, you know that I am a
great hunter, and that I have invented
many new devices in hunting which no other man
ever thought of; and you know also that I have
made improvements in the hoods and leashes, such
as were never made before ; nevertheless the people
speak ill of me, and ridicule me; and when they
praise the Cid Ruy Diaz, or Count Ferdinand
Gonzalez, for the many things which they did, or
the holy and happy King Ferdinand for the many
conquests which he gained, they say of me, with
ironical praise, that I also have done many great
things, alluding to the hoods and leashes. Now I
feel this irony very painful to me, and injurious to
my character; therefore, I pray you, advise me what

to do, so as to avoid being ridiculed for the good things I do."

" My lord," said Patronio, " in order that you may know what it behoves you to do in this case, I will, with your permission, relate what happened to a Moorish king of Cordova." The Count assented, and Patronio proceeded :—

" There was in Cordova a Moorish king, named Alhaquima, who governed his kingdom well: he studied to act with honour to himself and justice to others ; indeed, he did all that was required of good kings ; not only in guarding their kingdoms, but in augmenting their territories, with the view that they might receive the praises of their people ; and after death be remembered for their good deeds. Yet this king gave himself up to a life of luxury and enjoyment ; vice and disorder reigning in his palace. Now it happened as they played before him on an instrument which the Moors liked very much, and which they called Albogon, that the king perceived that it did not sound as well as it ought, so he took the instrument and made a hole at the lower part of it, but in the same direction as the other holes ; and since that time the Albogon has given a much better sound than before.

" Now although this cannot be considered but as an improvement, yet it was not an act suited to the dignity of a king—and so thought the people—for when they heard that the improvement was made by the king, they exclaimed in a ridiculing manner

in Arabic, 'Vahedezut Alhaquima,' which sig-
nifies, 'This is the work of King Alhaquima.' This
exclamation became so common all over the country
that it at last reached the ears of the king, who
begged to know why the people always used this
saying; but his attendants were anxious to avoid
answering his question. He however insisted on
being told the truth, and the signification of the expression; so they were compelled to tell him. When
he heard it he was very much grieved; but instead of
punishing those who related the origin of the saying,
he resolved to do some worthy deed, in order that
the people might be compelled to praise him de-
servedly.

"At this time the mosque of Cordova not being
yet finished, King Alhaquima did all that was necessary for its completion, and in this way it became
one of the most beautiful mosques the Moors had in
Spain,—glory to God! it is now a church, called
'Saint Mary of Cordova.'—It was dedicated, by
the 'good King Ferdinand,' to Saint Mary after he
had taken Cordova from the Moors.

"Now when the Moorish king had done so good a
work as that of finishing the mosque he said to himself, the people have hitherto ridiculed me for the
addition I made to the Albogon, (one of which
instruments he then held before him,) but now they
have reason for praising me, for have I not completed
the mosque of Cordova? From this time the Moors
ceased to speak in ridicule of him; and to this

day, when they wish to exalt a good act, say, 'It is as the work of King Alhaquima.'

"And you, my lord, if you feel displeased and unhappy because you are ridiculed for the improvements you have made in hoods and leashes and other things relating to the chase, study to do some noble and worthy deed suitable to your station."

Count Lucanor found this to be good advice, and acted accordingly, the result being that the people spoke well of him.

Don Juan, considering this to be a good example, caused it to be written in this book, and made these verses, which say :—

> If any good thou doest, how small soever,
> Let it be nobly done, for good deeds live for ever.

NOTE.

It would appear that in this narrative the author refers to Al Hakem II, who reigned in Cordova from 961 to 976. He was a man of peace and a cultivator of the Arts, like his noble father Abd' el Nahman III, who built the beautiful city of Medina al Zarah, on the banks of the Guadalquivir, if he did not finish, at any rate he appears to have done much towards a mosque which occupied more than one hundred years in its completion.

King Ferdinand III, mentioned in the text, was enthusiastic in obtaining from the Moors their splendid mosques, with the view of converting them into Christian Churches; it was thus in 1236, that he conquered Cordova, and replacing the crescent with the cross on the tower of the mosque, with grand processions, benedictions, and prayers, purified and dedicated it to the Virgin Mary.

It is an interesting fact that to this day, the saying, "It is as the work of King Alhaquima," is a "household word," in Spain, when praise is to be bestowed for any work or achievement.

CHAPTER II.

Treats of that which happened to Lorenzo Suarez Gallinato, and Garciperez of Vargas, and another knight.

NE day when Count Lucanor was conversing with his counsellor Patronio, he said:—"Patronio, it happens that I have a powerful king for an enemy; our quarrel has lasted so long that we have now resolved, for our future welfare, to terminate the war. Now, although we have thus agreed, nevertheless we are suspicious one of the other, and I am always on my guard; for, not only his people, but mine also, have been assassinated; and they send me, without ceasing, secret messengers informing me that my own life is in danger. Now, as I wish to be at peace, I entreat you to advise me how to act under these circumstances."

"Count Lucanor," replied Patronio, "the advice which I have to give you demands your serious attention, and for many reasons.

"Firstly:—Any man wishing to quarrel with you will be under the necessity of making great preparations, while he will endeavour to lead you, at the same time, to understand that he only desires to serve you, and while appearing to regret the injuries you have sustained, will doubtless let fall some remark such as will raise your suspicion, of which you must avail yourself by making the required preparations, although this very act not improbably may lead to the rupture.

" He, however, who advises you to take no precaution, believe me, is not your friend; but he who would say, ' Strengthen the walls of your fortress,' gives you a reason to believe that he does not desire to enjoy your possessions; he again who would say to you, 'You have too many friends and attendants, and you expend too much money in maintaining them,' gives you reason to believe that he does not like your honourable and secure position. So you see, you are in great danger if you take no measure of precaution, while again, if you do, you are very likely to bring about a conflict. But since you wish me to advise you how to act in this case, I will recount to you what happened to a certain very brave knight.

" The holy and good King Ferdinand, having besieged Seville, had amongst his followers three knights, who were considered the best and bravest in the world. One was Lorenzo Suarez Gallinato, another was Garciperez de Vargas, but the name of the other I have forgotten. These three knights had, one day, a dispute among themselves as to who was the most daring and valiant; and, since they could not agree in any other manner, they each determined to reach the gate of Seville, and to strike it with their

lances. The following morning they armed, and
rode towards the city. Now when the Moors who
were on the bastions and towers saw only three
knights, they thought that they came as envoys, so
allowed them to pass the moat, and parapet, and
arrive at the city gate. On reaching the gate, each
knight struck it with his lance, and having done so,
turned his horse's head towards the camp. When
the Moors saw the knights returning without leaving
any message, they concluded that they had come
only to offer an insult, and so determined to pursue
them. On opening the gate the Moors found that
the knights had already gone some distance; nevertheless they followed them with fifteen hundred
horse, and more than twenty thousand foot. Now
when the three knights saw the Moors approaching,
they turned their horses, and waited their arrival;
but, on their coming nearer, the knight, whose name
I have forgotten, was the first to charge them,
whilst Lorenzo Suarez and Garciperez remained
quiet; but, on the Moors coming still nearer, Garciperez charged them also, Lorenzo Suarez still
remaining stationary until the Moors forced him to
the attack; when he threw himself among them
and performed wonderful acts of valour. When
the royal army saw their knights surrounded by
the Moors, they hastened to their assistance, as they
saw them in great danger; but, by the mercy of
God, none of these knights were mortally (although
severely) wounded. The conflict, however, between

the Moors and Christians became so general that
king Ferdinand was obliged to approach in person;
and on that day the Christians displayed great valour.

"When the king returned to the camp, he ordered
these three knights to be brought before him, telling
them that they deserved death for having acted so
foolishly, by having without his orders brought on a
general engagement; thereby causing the loss of many
brave soldiers. The chiefs of the army, however,
interceded with the king for them, and they were
liberated in consequence.

"Soon after, the king, hearing that the knights had
acted from a spirit of emulation, ordered them to
attend again, and assembled all the most valiant men
of his army; so that they might decide which was
the bravest. The debate was animated, each bringing forth good reason for praising his own party—
some maintaining that he who first attacked the
Moors displayed the greatest courage;—others giving
preference to the second; the decision, however, was
given thus:—

"If the Moors who approached had not been so
numerous, and could skill and courage have conquered, then the knight who first charged them
only began that which he might have completed;
but, since this was not the case, he must have
approached, not to conquer, but, through shame of
flight, and an inability to resist the influence of fear,
therefore it was that he made the attack. The
second had better hopes than the first, because he

resisted acting in an hopeless cause and bore longer
the emotions consequent upon his perilous position.
But, Lorenzo Suarez Gallinato, who waited until the
Moors attacked him, was judged to be the most
valiant.

"And you, my lord, although you are kept in the
state of alarm and suspicion of which you now complain, yet engage not in a struggle the end of which
you cannot forsee, continue to exercise your good
sense, and do not suffer yourself to be led away
by false reports.   Your defences are good, so that,
even from a sudden attack, you cannot receive much
damage.

"I advise you now, my lord, to be of good
cheer, since you cannot be seriously injured.   Wait
before you act, for perhaps you will see that the reports which annoy you are not true.   Those who
create these alarms seek only their own interest;
and believe me, whether they be of your own or
your enemy's people, they are indifferent whether it
be war or peace; their object being only that they
may be favoured with an opportunity during the
commotion to gratify their wicked passions—so that,
during the conflict between you and your enemy,
they may possess themselves, not only of that belonging to yourself, but of that which belongs to others,
without fear of punishment.

"So that you are secured against any sudden attack,
it is much better to wait until the wrong comes from
the other side.   Be patient—all may yet end well—

God will be with you, which in such a cause is no small matter. Again, all people will know that you act only for your own preservation; nor can your enemy declare himself aggrieved. Thus may you preserve peace, which is agreeable to the will of God and all good men."

Don Juan, finding this to be a good example, wrote the following lines, which say :—

> When danger comes, haste not to meet it,
> Quietly wait, yet boldly treat it.

NOTES.

Of these three knights of the thirteenth century we have little on record. Don Lorenzo Suarez Gallinato has, however, been mentioned in another example, the forty-ninth chapter of this work, by Don Manuel, where he appears, although a Christian, to have occupied the distinguished post of Chief of the body-guard to the King of Granada.

Of Garcio Perez Vargas the genealogy has been carefully traced by Argote de Molina, in his Nobleza de Andalucia, fol. 96-122, where he is mentioned as one of the nobles of Count Don Pedro. The most brilliant part of his career was at the siege of Seville, and at the battle of Zeres, where he was knighted by the hand of Don Alvar Perez de Castro, for having killed the King of Ganzules. His name is perpetuated by an inscription still existing over the gate of Zeres at Seville, of which the following is a translation :—

> " Hercules built me,
> Julius Cæsar surrounded me with walls and lofty towers,
> A Gothic King lost me,
> The holy King won me,
> Assisted by Garcio Perez de Vargas."

The brother of this hero, Diego Perez de Vargas, is mentioned by Cervantes as a man of great prowess and valour Fighting bravely one day at the siege of Seville, against the Moors, he broke his sword, when seizing a heavy branch or trunk of an oak tree, he, with his terrible weapon, caused such destruction among his enemies that he was nicknamed "El Machaco (the Pounder,)" from the Spanish word Machacar, to pound. Since then the family have assumed the name and have been known as Vargas y Machacar (Don Quixote, cap. 8).

CHAPTER III.

Treats of that which happened to Don Rodrigo el Franco and his knights.

ONE day as Count Lucanor was conversing with Patronio his counsellor, he said:—"Patronio, it has happened that I have had many great wars, and of such a kind that I have often found myself much embarrassed. Upon one occasion I was in the greatest distress, when those to whom I have done much service, and who are indebted to me for all they possess, deserted me,—nay more, even exerted themselves to injure me. Such conduct, to tell you truly, has given me a worse opinion of mankind than I had before I knew these people: I therefore request your advice how to act under these circumstances."

"My lord," said Patronio, "if those people who

have acted so ungratefully were like Nuñez de
Fuente Almejir and Ruy Gonzalez de Zavallos and
Gutierre Rodriguez de Langueruella, and had known
what happened to them, they would not have acted
as they have done."

"How was that?" said the Count.

"My Lord," said Patronio, "it happened thus;—
The Count Rodrigo el Franco married a lady of
rank, daughter of Garcia de Azagra. This lady was
very virtuous; but the Count, her husband, calumniated her. Having no other resource, she prayed
to God that if she were guilty He would demonstrate
it by a miracle; and if the Count had falsely accused
her, He would show it also by a miracle. Scarcely
was the prayer ended, when, by a miracle of God,
the Count was smitten with leprosy, and she parted
from him. Soon after this separation, the King of
Navarre having sent his Ambassador to demand the
hand of the lady, she accepted him and became
Queen of Navarre. The Count being leprous, and
seeing that his disease could not be cured, made a
pilgrimage to the Holy Land that he might die
there. Now, although he had been much honoured
and had many faithful retainers, yet there accompanied him only the three knights of whom I have
spoken, who dwelt there so long that they expended
all they had brought from their own country, and
were reduced to such poverty that they had nothing
to give the Count to eat. Being so reduced, they
resolved that two of them should each day go to the

market-place for hire, while the other remained with
the Count,—and in this way they supported their
lord ; as also every night they bathed and wiped the
wounds of the leper.   It happened one night, as they
were bathing his arms and legs, that they felt inclined
to spit,—and so spat.   When the Count saw that all
spat, and believing that they did it from the disgust
which his malady created, he began to weep, greatly
regretting the dislike and repugnance which they
evinced towards him; when they, wishing to convince the Count that they felt no disgust, took up
in their hands some of the water, impure as it was,
and drank freely of it.   In this manner they continued devoted to the Count until he died.   They
then determined that it would be wrong to return
to Castille without the Count, living or dead ; so
they resolved to take his body with them.   The
distance making this difficult, the natives advised
them to boil the body and take the bones, but they
replied they would never consent to this, for as they
had not allowed any one to touch their lord during
his life, neither would they now that he was dead.
They then buried him, and waited patiently until
all the flesh had perished from off his bones, which
they collected, and placing them in a chest, carried
them back to Castille on their shoulders, begging
their food as they went, and although bearing
evident marks of their wretched poverty, arrived
nevertheless in good health at Tolosa.

"On one occasion, as they entered a city on their

way, they met a crowd of people who were leading
a lady of rank to be burned, she having been accused by her husband's brother of adultery, and the
sentence would be fulfilled unless a knight were
found who would defend her.

" Now, when Pero Nuñez, of noble and loyal
character, heard that, for want of a defender, she
might be lost, he told her relations that if he knew
the lady to be innocent he would save her, and he
requested the lady herself to reveal to him the whole
truth. She said she certainly had not committed the
crime of which they accused her, but that she had
had the intention of doing so. Pero Nuñez, on
hearing that she had had the intention to do what
she ought not, felt assured that some misfortune
would happen to whomsoever might defend her ; but
since he had already espoused her cause, and knew
that she had not committed the crime of which they
accused her, he declared himself her champion.
Her accusers attempted to prevent his interference
under the plea of his not being noble ; but Pero
Nuñez having proved his nobility, and that they
could not prevent him, the friends of the lady
furnished him with a horse and arms. Before
entering the arena he said to her friends, that, with
the assistance of God, he would save the lady and
return with honour, but that he felt assured some
harm would befall him for the evil which she had
intended doing.

"Soon after entering the arena, by the help of

God, Pero Nuñez vanquished his adversary and
saved the lady, but in doing so lost an eye,—and so
was that fulfilled which he had anticipated.

"The lady and her relations made so many presents to Pero Nuñez, that he and his two companions were able to pursue their journey with more
ease, still carrying the bones of their lord.

"As they were themselves without leprosy, the
King of Castille, hearing of their approach, and that
they were carrying with them the bones of their
master, expressed himself much gratified to have
amongst his subjects such faithful vassals. He sent,
therefore, a request that they should come direct to
him on foot, dressed just as they were. On the day
they returned to the kingdom of Castille, the King
himself went on foot five leagues beyond the
frontiers of his dominions to meet them. On their
arrival they received so many gifts from the King
and the people, that they not only became rich
themselves, but their descendants also after them.

"Now the King and all those who accompanied
him came to do honour to the memory of the
Count, but more especially to the devotion shown
by the three knights. They all followed the remains
of the leper until they arrived at Osma, where they
were interred, after which the three knights separated,
and each returned to his home.

"The day Ruy Gonzalez arrived at his house,
and was seated at table with his wife, she seeing the
good meat which was placed before her, raised her

hands to heaven, and said, 'Lord! blessed mayest thou be, that thou hast permitted me to see this day, for thou knowest that since Ruy Gonzalez departed from this country this is the first time that I have eaten meat or drunk wine;' and Ruy Gonzalez was grieved and said, 'Why have you done so?' Do 'you not remember,' said she, 'that when you departed with the Count, and vowed that you would not return without him, you expressed a wish that I should live as a good and honest wife, wanting not bread and water; and since you said that, would it have been right to disobey your wishes? and for this have I eaten only bread and water.'

"Pero Nuñez, arriving at his house, was received by his wife and friends with great joy, and so great was their pleasure that they could not look at him without laughing, so much so, that Pero Nuñez was impressed with the feeling that they laughed because he had lost an eye; so, with an air of chagrin, he covered his head with his cloak and threw himself on the bed. His good wife, seeing him so sad, was greatly afflicted, and so earnestly did she urge him to tell her the cause of his grief, that he was constrained to say he thought they laughed at him for having lost his eye. No sooner had she heard this than, seizing a needle, she thrust it in her own eye, thereby destroying it, and exclaiming,—'Henceforth if any one laughs it cannot be in contempt of you.' And so God rewarded these trusty knights for their fidelity and honour.

"And now, my lord, I say as before,—if those of whom you complain had been like these three knights, or had even known what happened to them, they would not have conducted themselves as they have done.

"But to you, Count Lucanor, permit me to say that the evil conduct of these people must not prevent you from doing good when it is in your power. It is not necessary to separate those to whom you have been serviceable from those you may have injured; but were you to do so, you would probably find that you have received more good from the first than evil from the latter. It would be foolish to expect gratitude from all men to whom you have rendered service ; but it might so happen that one of those people may so remunerate you with his devotion, as would compensate you for all the good you have done to others."

The Count estimated this as a wise and virtuous precept. And it being considered by Don Juan as a narrative worthy to be retained, he ordered it to be written in this book, and made these lines :—

> Though others injure thee, or spite,
> Yet cease not thou to do aright.

NOTES.

Although each age and country may have its distinguishing glory, whether it be the wisdom of Athens, the arts of Greece, or the heroism of Rome, or the chivalry of the Crusaders, none is perhaps more attractive in its character than the last-named, and it is in this that Don Manuel has depicted that patient and devoted fidelity displayed by his three knights to their degraded and expatriated lord, in which their feudal honour and allegiance knew no check until their mission was completely fulfilled. The little interlude of gallantry displayed by Pero Nuñez, so neatly introduced, showing that even an evil intention not carried into effect brings with it always a certain punishment, demands our approval.

The names and chivalric deeds of these three knights have been handed down to posterity in the Nobiliare of Argote de Molina.

CHAPTER IV.

Of a Hermit who fought to know whom he should have for his companion in Paradise, and of the leap made by King Richard of England.

NE day Count Lucanor having called Patronio, said to him, "Patronio, I have great faith in your understanding, and believe that in any matter which you could not comprehend or give advice about no other man could succeed; I beg therefore that you will advise me as best you can on that which I am now going to tell you.

"You know very well that I am no longer young and that I have been engaged all my life in one war or another; sometimes against the Christians, at other times the Moors, or kings to whom I owe allegiance, and again, with my more powerful neighbours. Now, whenever I chanced to be engaged against the Christians I always carefully avoided, as far as possible, being the aggressor; nevertheless, it was difficult to act without sometimes inflicting serious damage on many who did not deserve it. Now, for these and the other sins which I have committed, I know I shall one day have to answer; and as death is certain, and at my age cannot be very far distant, I desire, while I have yet time, to obliterate by good works and deeds of penance my numerous offences, so that, when I appear in the presence of God, I may be worthy of His mercy and a place in Paradise. I pray you, Patronio, as you know how I have hitherto lived, to counsel me now how to act, so as to make reparation for past errors, and attain the happy end I so ardently desire."

"My lord," said Patronio, "I am much pleased at all you have just told me, particularly for the permission you have given me to advise you concerning your present state of life; had I less confidence in your friendship I might think you merely sought to prove me as the king did his favourite, the history of which I related to you the other day. But I am most pleased to see you really desire to make reparation for the sins you have committed against God, without however renouncing your duties or sacrificing your honour; for certainly, were you to retire from the world and become a monk, you would be guilty of one or both of the above-named faults.

"Firstly, people would say that you were deficient in judgment or courage to be contented merely to live useless amongst the good men of this century; and secondly, it would surprise me very much if you could endure the continued asperities of a monkish life, which, if you were afterwards to forsake or continue to live therein, careless of fulfilling or forgetful of the duties of your state, it would be a very serious injury to your soul, a dishonour to your name, and a blot on your reputation.

"But since you have formed the good resolution to save your soul, permit me to recount to you what God revealed to a very holy hermit, as also what happened to him and King Richard of England."

"I pray you," replied the Count, "to inform me of these particulars."

"My lord," said Patronio, "there was a hermit who led a very good life, and who laboured much, enduring many hardships for the glory of God, insomuch that God in His great mercy and grace promised him that he should be admitted to the glory of Paradise.

"The hermit thanked God very sincerely and on this point was well satisfied, but prayed that yet another favour might be granted him, which was that he might see who was to be his companion in

Paradise. The Lord made known to him by an angel that he ought not to ask these questions; but so earnest were his prayers, that God thought well to send one of his heavenly spirits a second time to inform him that he should have Richard, King of England, for his companion in Paradise.

"Although this revelation pleased the hermit, yet it very much astonished him, for he knew King Richard, and also that he was a great warrior, causing the death of many innocent people, and pillaging towns and driving the inhabitants into exile; now that this man was to be his companion in Paradise, having always led a life so contrary to his, appeared passing strange, as he had always thought King Richard very far removed from the road to salvation.

"The Lord seeing his little faith, again sent an angel to tell him not to doubt, but to believe implicitly that which had been revealed to him.

"'Know you not,' said the angel, 'that King Richard has done no less service to God than your-self, and equally merits Paradise in reward for his leap, as you do for all the good works performed during your life.' Now this information only increased the astonishment of the hermit, who wondered what this could be.

"The angel replied thus, 'The Kings of France, of Navarre, and of England joined in the crusade beyond seas; when they arrived at the port they saw, as they prepared to land, so large a multitude of

Moors on the coast that they feared being able to
disembark.   It was then that the King of France
sent to the King of England who was already on
horseback.   On hearing what the envoy had to say,
and that the King of France desired his presence on
board his ship to counsel together as to what was
best to be done, he replied, That for his part
his resolution was taken, come what might; feeling
very sensible that he had often failed in the due
performance of his duty to God, and had committed
many sins in this world, nevertheless he had always
prayed for forgiveness and that an opportunity might
be granted him during his life to make amends;
now he praised God, for he saw the way he had
long hoped for, since, if he was killed, being truly
penitent, he felt certain that for what he was about
to do God would pardon his manifold sins; and
if, on the contrary, the Moors were conquered, it
would be rendering a great service to God; so
that, come what would, all was for the best.

" 'And, having said this, he commended his body
and soul to God, and praying for His holy protection,
made the sign of the Cross, and ordering his soldiers
to follow him, stuck his spurs into his horse and
jumped into the sea facing the coast where the
Moors were assembled; this being near the port,
the sea was very deep, yet the king and his horse
did not disappear.

" ' But God, as a merciful Lord and full of power,
remembering what He had said in the Gospel, "That

He did not desire the death of a sinner, but rather that he should be converted and live," helped the King of England, and saved him from the death of this world, so that he escaped the perils of the sea. The English, seeing this brave act of their king, followed him into the water and joined him in battle against the Moors.

" 'When the Navarrais and French saw this they felt ashamed to remain on board their ships, and, not being accustomed to endure disgrace, jumped also into the sea and joined in the conflict. The Moors seeing them approach, and admiring this brave contempt of danger, durst not wait for them, but abandoned the port and fled towards the country, but many were overtaken and killed. The Christians were very prosperous and gained much glory for God, all of which resulted from the brave leap made by King Richard of England!'

"When the hermit heard this he was well pleased, and saw how that God favoured him in permitting him to be the companion in Paradise of a man who had done so well in the service of God and in exalting the Catholic Faith.

"And you, Count Lucanor, if you wish to serve God and obtain forgiveness of your sins, try, before you leave this earth, to make amends for the wrongs which you have done to others, be penitent for your sins without taking thought for the things of this world, which are but vanity. Take no heed of those who may say your acts are but to obtain worldly

credit, nor of those who would engage you in
unworthy enterprises to gratify your self-love, by
which much evil is committed ; for, after all, what is
ambition ? Far from following such a course, full
of peril, direct your energies so that you may merit
eternal life, and as it has pleased God to place you
in a country where you can fight against the Moors,
both by sea and land, so also let all your efforts be
directed to the service of your country, being sure
that, having made amends to God for the sins you
have committed, and being truly penitent, you will
undoubtedly receive the reward for the good which
you have done and will do, together with complete
forgiveness, so that you can rest satisfied in the
service of God even to the end of your days. This,
I think, is the best plan you can adopt for the salvation of your soul and the preservation of your estates
and honour ; and should you be slain while in the
service of God, your death will be that of a martyr :
also, should you die when in the enjoyment of peace,
you will be blessed for the good works you have
done ; nor could any man speak ill of you, for all
would know that you have done everything required
of an honourable knight and a faithful servant of
God, and that you had ceased to be a slave of the
devil, abstaining from all the vanities of this world,
which are so deceitful.

"And now, Count Lucanor, I have given you my
advice as you have demanded, and have instructed
you how to save your soul in your present state of

life ; hold fast your good resolutions, and you will resemble King Richard of England in the leap which he made."

And the Count was well pleased with the counsels which Patronio gave him, and prayed that an opportunity might be granted to him in like manner to serve God as he desired in his heart.

And Don Juan saw that this example was very good, and ordered it to be written in this book, and composed the following lines :—

> So shall a man reach, by a leap, to heaven,
> Obeying trustfully the laws that God hath given.

NOTES.

The wild project of Peter the Hermit, which roused all Europe to arms in the 11th century, has been a fruitful source of laudatory prose and verse even to the present day ; nor has it, as we see, escaped the versatile genius of our author, Don Manuel, who, in this chapter, has not only illustrated the heroism and self-devotion of the age, but has also depicted the Pharisaism of the hermit, recalling to our minds also, in the record of the heroic leap of Richard Cœur de Lion, the parable of Jesus, wherein the householder rewards the workman of the eleventh hour, saying to him who murmured, "Take that thine is, and go thy way ; I will give unto this last even as unto thee."

CHAPTER V.

Of that which happened to the Emperor Frederick and Don Alvar Fañez, with their wives.

OUNT LUCANOR, conversing one day with his counsellor Patronio, said, "I have two brothers who are married and maintain in their establishments a conduct entirely different. One is so enamoured of his wife as to be unable to leave her a single minute; he does only that which she wishes, and never decides on anything whatever without first having taken her advice. The other, on the contrary, allows nothing to be done but what he wishes; we cannot persuade him to live with his wife, or even take any notice of her. I am afflicted, equally, to find so much weakness in the one and so much aversion in the other. Tell me, then, I pray you, the means, if there be any, to remedy such a state of things."

"My lord," replied Patronio, "you are right in saying your brothers are equally to blame; but what can you do? The influence of women is very powerful, and often urges us to do wrong to please them. Nevertheless, I would desire you to hear what happened to the Emperor Frederick and to Don Alvar Fañez with their wives, which I think you will find not to be without application to this case."

" Willingly," said the Count. And Patronio proceeded as follows :—

" As I have two histories to recount, and cannot
tell you both at once, I will first relate that of the
Emperor Frederick, and then pass on to that of Don
Alvar Fañez. The Emperor Frederick married a
lady of very high position and birth, suitable to his
rank ; but still they were not happy, for he knew
not before the marriage her real character. But
after their union (although she was a very virtuous
woman), she became the most daring, violent, and
perverse person in the world ; for if the Emperor
desired to eat, she desired to fast ; if he wished to
sleep, it would be her wish to arise ; everything in
which the Emperor took pleasure was to her an
object of aversion, and all his desires she opposed
by doing exactly the contrary. The Emperor
suffered this state of things a long time, and felt
that he was unable to better his position ; for
neither prayers, persuasions, nor even threats,
availed anything: good and bad treatment were
alike unsuccessful. His whole life was made miserable, and he became perplexed as to what he should
do, as much for his people as for himself. At last
he resolved to appeal to the Pope, and related to
him all his troubles respecting the conduct of the
Empress, begging that he would agree to their
separation.

" 'I see,' said the Pope, ' that, according to the
Christian religion, a separation cannot be permitted ;

yet, on the other hand, it is impossible to live with
the Empress, in consequence of her violent temper.
What can be done? The Supreme Law does not
permit me to inflict penance unless actual sin has
been committed; but I leave you at liberty to act as
you consider most wise and convenient.'

"The Emperor, after hearing the Pope's opinion,
was very much concerned how to act; whether by
persuasion, reasoning, or kindness, so as to remedy
the present state of things. But still he found all
his efforts of no avail; the more he strove to obtain
peace, the more perverse the Empress became.

"Now, as the Emperor saw that nothing could be
done, he one day expressed a wish to go stag-hunt-
ing, and made a poisonous preparation of herbs to
put on the arrows, thereby rendering the wound fatal.
Putting away a part of this preparation to be in readiness for another hunt, he requested the Empress not
to touch it on any account whatever, whether for the
itch or any unhealed eruption; for, said he, 'it is
so very poisonous that it would destroy any living
thing; but here is another ointment, very excellent
and much approved of.' The Emperor then applied
some of the latter to heal some spots which he had,
so that all present might bear witness to its utility in
curing such complaints. All this was done in the
presence of the knights and ladies there assembled,
after which he departed for the chase.

"Now, the Empress, who had heard him in
silence, laughed, and said, 'What deceit; I know

well that our ailments are different, and he has
recommended me to use this ointment which he
employs because it cannot cure me; but I am not so
foolish, I will use the forbidden ointment, and on
his return he will find me well, and this, I know,
will enrage him; so much the better—it is another
reason for my using it.'

"All who were present tried to dissuade the
Empress, both by their tears and supplications.
'Your death is certain,' said they, 'if that poison is
used.' But all without avail. For scarcely had she
applied the ointment when her agony—and with it,
her regret—commenced. But it was too late;
nothing could save her. Thus she died, a victim to
her own perverse disposition.

"But to Don Alvar Fañez it happened quite
otherwise. And, in order that you may understand
the whole, I will now recount his history to you.

"Alvar Fañez was a very good man, and was
much honoured. He colonized the village of Ysca,
where he resided, together with Count Pero Anzurez,
who had with him three daughters.

"One day Don Alvar Fañez paid an unexpected
visit to the Count, who, nevertheless, expressed
himself much gratified, and, after they had dined
together, desired to be informed the cause of his
unexpected visit. Don Alvar Fañez replied that he
came to demand one of his daughters in marriage,
and requested permission to see the three ladies, that
he might speak to each of them separately, when he

would select the one he should desire in marriage. Now the Count, feeling that God would bless that proposition, agreed to it.

"So Don Alvar Fañez, taking aside the eldest daughter, said that, if it was agreeable to her, he desired to marry her; but, before pursuing his suit, begged to recount to her something concerning himself which she ought to know. 'I am,' said he, 'not very young, and, in consequence of many wounds received by me in various conflicts, my intellects have become weakened; when I drink a little wine, I know not what I say or do, and am often very violent, but regret all this very sincerely on coming to my senses; also, I am much troubled in my sleep, and suffer from various other causes; indeed, so much so that few women would consent to marry me.' When he had said this, the daughter of the Count replied, 'The marriage does not depend on me, but on my parents.'

"On hearing this reply Don Alvar Fañez returned to her father, who inquired of his daughter, if the proposed alliance was agreeable to her, and found that, since the interview, she would rather die than marry him. The Count, not wishing to explain the cause, simply said his daughter did not wish to marry.

"Don Alvar Fañez then had an interview with the second daughter, when he spoke in the same manner as he had done to the first; and it produced the same result. He then repeated to the youngest daughter all he had said to the two others. She replied, however, that she thanked God very much that Don Alvar Fañez desired to marry her; and as to what he had said about the wine making him ill, should it happen at any time when he was apart from his attendants, she would assist him better than any other person in the world. With respect to his age, she would not decline on that account, but was satisfied with the honour of being his wife. And as to his being furious and rough with his people, she would take care not to excite him, and if hurt herself she knew how to suffer. And to all the things which Don Alvar Fañez said, she replied so favourably that he was very well satisfied, and thanked God that he had found a woman with such an understanding, and told the Count, her father, that he desired to marry this his youngest daughter, whose name was Vascuñana. The Count and his wife were much gratified at this announcement, and quickly made arrangements for the marriage.

" After the marriage, Don Alvar Fañez returned home with his wife, whom he found to be so good a housekeeper and so prudent that he considered himself very fortunate in marrying her, and therefore resolved to do only that which was agreeable to her, because God had given her so many good qualities and an excellent understanding. She, on her part, loved her husband very much, and felt that all he did or said was right and for the best. She never disapproved of or contradicted him in that which she

knew to be agreeable to him; nor did he think she
flattered, or acted with a view to deceive him, and
so gain his esteem. For this reason, Don Alvar
Fañez loved his wife, and regarded her as one whose
honour and care for his interests he had no reason to
doubt.

"It happened one day when Don Alvar Fañez
was at home, there came to visit him a nephew of
his who was attached to the King's household.
After he had been in the house some days, he said
to Don Alvar Fañez, 'You are a good and accomplished man, but there is one fault I find with
you.' His uncle desired to know what it was.
To which the nephew replied, 'It may be but a
small fault, but it is this, you study your wife too
much, and make her too great a mistress of you and
your affairs.'

"'As to that,' Don Alvar Fañez replied, 'I will
give you an answer in a few days.'

"After this, Don Alvar Fañez made a journey on
horseback to a distant part of the country, taking
with him his nephew, where he remained some
time, and then sent for his wife Vascuñana to meet
him on the road as he returned. When they had
journeyed some time without conversing, Don Alvar
Fañez being in advance, they chanced to meet a large
drove of cows, when Don Alvar said to his nephew,
'See what famous mares we have in this country.'

"The nephew, on hearing this, was surprised,
and thought he said it in jest, and asked him how he

could say so when they were but cows.   At this, his
uncle feigned to be quite astonished, saying, 'You are
mistaken, or have lost your wits, for they certainly
are mares.'   The nephew, seeing his uncle persist in
what he had said, and that, too, with so much
energy, became alarmed and thought his uncle had
lost his understanding.   The dispute, however, continued in this manner until they met Doña Vascuñana, who was now seen on the road approaching
them.   No sooner did Don Alvar Fañez perceive
his wife, than he said to his nephew, 'Here is my
wife, Vascuñana, who will be able to settle our dispute.'

"The nephew was glad of this opportunity, and
no sooner did she meet them than he said, 'Aunt,
my uncle and I have a dispute.   He says that those
cows are mares; I say they are cows.   And we
have so long contended this point, that he considers
me as mad, while I think he is but little better.   So
we beg you will settle our dispute.'

"Now when Doña Vascuñana heard this, although
they appeared to her to be cows, yet, as her husband had said to the contrary, and she knew that
no one was better able than he to distinguish one
from the other, and that he never erred, she, trusting entirely to his judgment, declared they were,
beyond all doubt, mares, and not cows.   'It grieves
me much, nephew,' continued Vascuñana, 'to hear
you contest the point; and God knows it is a great
pity you have not better judgment, with all the ad-

vantages you have had in living in the King's household, where you have been so long, than not to be
able to distinguish mares from cows.' She then began
to show how, both in their colour and form, and in
many other points, they were mares and not cows ;
and that what Don Alvar had said was true. And
so strongly did she affirm this, that not only her
nephew, but those who were with them began to
think they were themselves mistaken.

"After this Don Alvar Fañez and his nephew
proceeded. They had not, however, journeyed long
before they saw a large drove of mares. 'Now
these,' said Don Alvar Fañez, 'are cows, but those
we have seen, which you call cows, were not so.'

"When the nephew heard this, he exclaimed,
'Uncle, for God's sake ! if what you say be true,
the devil has brought me to this country ; for certainly, if these are cows, then have I lost my senses,
for in all parts of the world these are mares, and
not cows.' But Don Alvar persisted that he was right
in saying they were cows and not mares. And thus
they argued until Vascuñana came up to them, when
they related to her what had been said between them.

"Now, although she thought her nephew right,
yet, for the same reasons as before, she said so much
in support of her husband, and that, too, with such
apparent truth and inward conviction, that the
nephew and those with the mares began to think that
their sight and judgment erred and that what Don
Alvar had said was true ; and so the debate ended.

" Again Don Alvar and his nephew proceeded on their road homewards, and had proceeded a considerable distance when they arrived at a river, on the banks of which were a number of mills. While their horses were drinking, Don Alvar remarked that the river ran in the direction from which it flowed, and that the mills received their water from the contrary point. When the nephew heard this, he thought to a certainty he himself had lost his senses, for as he appeared to be wrong with respect to the mares and cows, so might he be in error here also, and the river might really run towards and not from its source. Nevertheless he contended the point. When Vascuñana, on her arrival, found them again warmly disputing, she begged to know the cause. They then informed her ; when, although, as before, it appeared to her that the nephew was right, yet she could not be persuaded that her husband was wrong, and so again supported his opinion ; and this time with so many good arguments, that the nephew and those present felt they must have been in error. And it remains a proverb to this day that, ' If the husband affirms that the river runs up to its source, the good-wife ought to believe it, and say that it is true.'

" Now when the nephew had heard all this, supposing that Don Alvar Fañez must be right, he began to feel very unhappy, and to suspect that he was losing his senses.

" Still pursuing their journey Don Alvar Fañez

observed his nephew to be very sad and depressed, so said to him, 'Now, nephew, understand that I have given you an answer to what you said to me the other day, when you and others blamed me for having so much confidence in my wife Vascuñana. All that you have seen to-day I have done in order that you might become acquainted with her real character, and that consequently my trust in her is not misplaced. I knew very well that the animals we first found, and which I called mares, were really cows, as you said ; and when Doña Vascuñana arrived and heard that I said they were mares I knew certainly that she thought you were right, but because she had confidence in me, and thought it impossible for me to err, gave it as her opinion that you were wrong respecting the animals and the river, and that too with such apparent good reasons. And I tell you truly that, from the day we were married, she has not done one thing to disoblige me ; she believes that I always judge and act for the best, wishes all the people to understand that I am the master, and arranges all things so that I may take pleasure in them. So now, nephew, you have the answer which I promised you the other day, when you reproached me with the fault of confiding too much in my wife.'

"The nephew, having heard these reasons, declared himself much pleased ; and seeing how trusting Doña Vascuñana was, and in what esteem she held her husband, he acknowledged Don Alvar was not on

his part too considerate and loving. Thus you see
how different were the wives of the Emperor and
Don Alvar Fañez.

"And so, Count Lucanor, if your brothers are so
different, the one doing all his wife desires and the
other doing quite the contrary, it is perhaps because
their wives are like the Empress and Doña Vascuñana.
And, if such is the case, you cannot wonder at nor
blame them for their conduct; but if it is not so,
then indeed your brothers are wrong, one for con-
ceding too much to his wife, who does not merit it,
the other for estranging himself from his wife, who
deserves his affection. But there is a limit to even
this, no man should so indulge his wife in all her
desires as to forsake his duty or honour. His love
must be tempered with discretion, and not the one
sacrificed to the other. Again, he should carefully
avoid being too fastidious in that which is unim-
portant or of no concern to him, for it is wrong to
be too particular about trifles and foster a spirit of
irritation and annoyance; also, the frequent necessity
of arranging these ridiculous quarrels tends only
to injure the honourable feelings and reputation of
both. Also, if any man should have such a wife as
the Emperor's, and, like him, be unable to remedy
his position, to him I can give no advice but to
place his trust in Providence. But you know it is
important to both that a man, from the day of his
marriage, should give his wife to understand that he

himself is the master, so that she may know the life she has to pass.

"And you, Count Lucanor, after what I have related, will be able now to advise your brothers how to act with their wives."

The Count was much pleased with what Patronio had told him, and found that what he had said was true and much to the purpose.

And Don Juan, considering these as good examples and worthy to be retained, ordered them to be written in this book; and made these lines, which say,—

> A man at his marriage should teach his wife
> How he intends her to pass her life.

NOTES.

The Count Don Alvar Fañez Minaya, referred to in this narrative, was cousin to the famous Cid, Ruy Diaz de Vivar. His mother was Doña Ximena Nunez, who married Fernan Laynez, brother of Diego Laynez, father of the Cid.

Pero Anzurés was the founder of the Church of Valladolid in 1095.—*Noblesa de Andalusia*, p. 104.

CHAPTER VI.

*Of that which happened to the Count of Provence
and Saladin the Sultan of Babylon.*

NE day, as Count Lucanor and Patronio
were conversing, the Count said :—

"Patronio, one of my vassals informed me the other day that he was
anxious to get one of his relations married, and
wished to consult me as to what was best to be
done, so begged me to favour him with my advice.
He informed me of all the conditions to be fulfilled
for this marriage. Now, as he is a man who I am
desirous should succeed in the world, and as I
know you have a good knowledge of such things,
I beg you will tell me how you think he should
act, so that I may be enabled to give him such
advice as shall be for his good."

"My lord," said Patronio, "in order that you
may be enabled to advise this man wisely I shall
be happy to recount, with your permission, that
which happened to the Count of Provence with
Saladin, Sultan of Babylon."

The Count requested Patronio to tell him what
that was ; so he said :—

"My lord, there was a Count in Provence who was a very good man and who desired to live so that God might have mercy on his soul, and purchase by his good actions the glory of Paradise. In order to accomplish this he made a pilgrimage to the Holy Land, taking with him a great number of his dependants well-provisioned; feeling in his heart that whatever happened to him would be fortunate, inasmuch as he had devoted himself to the service of God. But the ways of God are marvellous and inscrutable, and He sees good to place heavy temptations in the way of His servants; yet, if the temptation be resisted from the love to God, it will prove always to the honour and advantage of the tempted; thus it was that our Lord held it good to tempt the Count of Provence, and permitted him to be taken prisoner by the Sultan of Babylon.

"Saladin, hearing the high reputation which the Count enjoyed, showed him much attention, and treated him honourably. In all his great undertakings he consulted his prisoner, and followed his advice. Such was the confidence in the Count that, although nominally a prisoner, the people so respected him that in all the dominions of the Sultan he felt almost as if he were in his own kingdom.

"When the Count left his country he had a very young daughter who, during her father's long absence, had grown up and was now marriageable, upon which the Countess and her relations sent to inform the Count that many princes and great men had sought her in marriage. So, one day, when Saladin came to converse with the Count, the latter spoke to him in the following manner :—

"'My lord, you have granted me many favours and have shown me much consideration; this I feel a great honour, and, as you have deigned to consult me in many things, I pray your forgiveness if I now solicit your advice in a subject which deeply interests me.'

"The Sultan was gracious and said he would advise him with great pleasure and assist him in anything whatever it might be. The Count then informed him of the proposals made for his daughter's hand, when Saladin replied as follows :—

"'Count, I know your understanding to be such that with a few words you will be able to comprehend the subject entirely. You tell me of all those who claim your daughter's hand, their lineage and power, and their relationship with you, but as I do not know their habits and customs, and what advantages the one possesses over the other, I can only advise you to marry your daughter to a worthy man.'

"The Count thanked the Sultan, and sent word to the Countess and his relations, telling them what the Sultan had said, and that he wished to know all the particulars respecting the men and noblemen who were in the country, their habits and dispositions; and told them also that they must put in writing the qualities possessed by the princes and men of high rank who demanded his daughter. The Countess and the Count's relations were much astonished, but did as the Count desired, and wrote in detail all the good and bad habits which distinguished those who aspired to an alliance with the Count; and related to him everything respecting the noblemen who inhabited the country round about.

"The Count, on receiving this reply, showed it to the Sultan, who found it a satisfactory report, except that the princes and noblemen had each some one fault or another either in their eating and drinking, or that they were irritable or morose, had a bad address, associated with low company, were in debt, or had some other failing. But one, the son of a very rich man, who, although not so powerful as the others, according to what was written, was, in the Sultan's opinion, the most suitable man, and so he recommended the Count to marry his daughter to that man; for, although he understood the others to be more noble, it was better to esteem a man for his conduct than for his rank.

"The Count now sent to request the Countess and his relatives to marry his daughter as Saladin had suggested. Although they were much surprised at this advice of the Count, they nevertheless sent for that son of the rich man and told him what the Count required, who replied that he knew well that the Count was nobler, richer, and more honoured than himself; if, therefore, the proposition was made in jest they did him injustice, for he thought himself worthy to marry the Count's daughter or any other lady. They replied they wished it seriously, and recounted to him how the Sultan had advised the Count, who would now give his daughter to him in preference to any of the princes or great noblemen who sought her, because he considered him the most worthy man.

"Now when the rich man's son heard this he understood that they spoke in earnest of the marriage, and determined, since Saladin had chosen him from among so many other men, and done him so much honour, he would not fail in this case to do all that which, as an honourable man, was required of him ; he therefore called the Countess and the relations of the Count and told them, as he believed they had spoken truly, he desired to be put in entire possession of the estates of the Count and to receive all the rents, but he did not speak of his future intentions. They were, however, satisfied, and placed all things at his immediate command. As soon as he found himself master of a large sum of money he armed a galley, and requested that the marriage should be solemnized on a particular day.

"When night came and the ceremony was ended with all its splendour and honour, he called together the Countess, his mother-in-law, and all their relations, and said, 'You know very well that the Count has chosen me from amongst many others as the best man, by the advice of the Sultan. Having, therefore, been so much honoured, I feel called upon to act so as to prove myself worthy of my election. I therefore intend leaving home immediately, and recommend to your charge the young lady, my wife, and all the estates ; for I feel confident that God will assist me, and all the world shall know that I have done my duty.'

"Soon after this the young man departed on horseback, full of hope, and travelled till he arrived at the kingdom of Armenia, where he remained until he knew the language and habits of the people well, by which time he discovered that Saladin was fond of hunting ; so having the very best hawks and dogs possible, he went in his galley to meet Saladin. Putting into a secure harbour, he commanded his men not to leave that spot without his orders. When he came to where Saladin was, he was well received by him, but he did not kiss his hand, nor offer the homage which was due to him as the Sultan, yet Saladin ordered all his wants to be attended to. The young man thanked him much, declaring that he required nothing, and that he came only, having heard of his great renown in the chase, to beg that he might be permitted to join in his retinue, in order that he might enjoy the advantage of his experience and that of his people. Having brought with him many excellent birds and dogs, he besought the Sultan to select from them those he wished, and with what remained to him begged permission to join in the hunt, where he would render every

service. This offer pleased the Sultan much, and
he made the selection as desired, but regretted that
his guest could not be induced to receive anything
in return.

"After some time it pleased God that things
should happen as this young man desired. The
falcons chased a crane in the direction of the port
where he had anchored his galley. The Sultan rode
a very good horse, as did also his guest, when they
found themselves far from the retinue, none of whom
knew the direction they had taken. On Saladin
arriving where the falcons had caught the crane he
dismounted in haste and ran to assist them. His
young companion, seeing him on the ground occupied in feeding the falcons, called his men. Now
when the Sultan saw the people from the galley
around him, and that the young man had drawn
his sword upon him, he was much astonished, and
exclaimed, 'It is a base treason.'

"'God forbid!' said the other; 'you know I
never did homage to you as my lord, neither have
I accepted anything from you.' He had this reason
for not doing so. Having said this, he took him
and put him on board the galley, telling him that
he was the son-in-law of the Count whom he, the
Sultan, had chosen as the man worthy to be married
to the Count's daughter; and since he had so chosen
him, he felt that he would not do credit to his judgment unless he acted as he had done. The young
man then prayed the Sultan to deliver up to him

his father-in-law, saying, 'So shall it be known that the advice you have given me was indeed good and wise.'

"When Saladin heard this, he was much pleased, and thanked God, being better satisfied that his advice had succeeded than if it had happened otherwise, and told the son-in-law that he would deliver up his father-in-law with great pleasure.

"The young man, having confidence in the Sultan's word, put him on shore, and accompanied him, but ordering his people from the galley to retire so that they should not be seen by those who might arrive.

"The Sultan and the son-in-law were feeding the falcons when the suite arrived. They found their master in good humour, but he told none of them what had happened to him.

"As soon as they arrived at the city, the Sultan went down to the house where the Count was a prisoner, taking with him the son-in-law. When the Sultan saw the Count, he began by saying with much gaiety, 'Count, I thank God for His mercy in having prospered so well the advice which I gave as to the marriage of your daughter. Behold your son-in-law, who has been the means of releasing you from prison.' He then related all that the son-in-law had done; his loyalty and the great efforts he had made to liberate him, as also the implicit confidence he had in his, the Sultan's, word.

"Now, the Count, and all who heard this, praised

4

the son-in-law very much for his judgment, valour, and great energy; while some praised the Sultan for his great goodness, and thanked God who had directed all things for so good an end.

"The Sultan gave the Count and his son-in-law many rich presents. To the Count he gave double the amount of the rents which he would have received from his estates during the time of his captivity; and thus sent him away very rich and much honoured to his own country.

"Now all this good fortune befell the Count through the good advice which the Sultan gave him respecting the marriage of his daughter with one deserving to be called a *man*.

"And you, my lord, since you have to advise one of your vassals respecting the marriage of one of his relatives, tell him that the principal thing is to marry her to a *good man;* for, if not, no matter how rich, honourable, or mighty he may be, she can never be well married. And you ought to know that a man by his good actions increases the honour, elevates the position of his family, and augments his riches. Of this I could give you many examples. Men of good position, whose fathers were rich and much respected, but who themselves were not as good as they ought to be, have lost both their position and riches. Others, of humbler rank, by their great goodness have gained for themselves riches and honour, so as to become much more respected and esteemed for their conduct than for their lineage.

"And so you will now understand that all the good and evil which befalls us arises from our own actions, let a man's rank be what it may. Therefore, the first thing you ought to inquire after is, what are the habits, the understanding, and general conduct of the man himself, or of the woman, who is about to marry; and these being, in the first place, satisfactory, then, the higher the rank, the greater the riches, and the more honourable the position of the connection, the better."

The Count was much pleased with the reasons which Patronio gave him, and held as true all that he had spoken.

Don Juan, seeing that this example was very good, wrote it in this book, and made this verse, which says :—

> The upright man, in all he does, prevails ;
> The wicked, in his plans, as surely fails.

NOTE.

Calderon has made the above story the subject of a three-act comedy, entitled "Count Lucanor." It would seem likely, at first sight, that in giving this name to the bold knight who seized on the person of Saladin, his object was to recall, by an ingenious transposition, the collection to which he was indebted for the idea of the piece. But, as he concludes his drama by asking pardon for a history drawn from the books of chivalry, there seems to be some force in the opinion maintained by Ticknor, that Count Lucanor was a name borrowed from one of those old books of knight-errantry, and adopted by Don Manuel to avoid the possibility of his being supposed, in the name of his hero, to indicate any veritable living contemporary of his. Indeed had Calderon been acquainted with Don Manuel's story, he could hardly have departed so widely as he has done from its moral application. In his comedy, no train of thought or moral lesson is enforced : his sole object appears to have been to complicate with romantic incidents one of those adventures which the heroes of chivalry prided themselves in bringing to a happy termination.

The Sultan Saladin plays an important part in the tales and Fabliaux of the middle ages. Don Juan Manuel has himself introduced him more than once in this book. He was the Alexander of the Crusades—this Salehaddin, who, after having been in the service of the Sultans of Egypt, usurped their throne, became a famous conqueror, and, by the resplendent lustre of his virtues and magnanimity, palliated the cruelties indispensable to his victories, and obtained the title of *Great*—a title more gloriously consecrated by the *Gerusalemme* of Tasso than by all the panegyrics of historians.

CHAPTER VII.

Of that which happened to a King and three Impostors.

COUNT LUCANOR, conversing at another time with Patronio, his adviser, said :—

"Patronio, a man came to me and told me something, giving me to understand it would be of great advantage to me if I followed his suggestions ; but he said no man must be informed of the secret, that I must trust in him, and, more than this, affirmed that if I should confide it to any man in the world I should place not only my property but my life in danger. And as I know no man able to detect a fraud so quickly as yourself I pray you give me your opinion in this case."

"My lord," said Patronio, "in order that you may know how to act under these circumstances, it would please me to be permitted to inform you what happened to a King and three impostors."

The Count requested to know what that was.

"My lord," said Patronio, "three impostors came to a King, and told him they were cloth-weavers, and could fabricate a cloth of so peculiar a nature that a legitimate son of his father could see the cloth; but if he were illegitimate, though believed to be legitimate, he could not see it.

"Now the King was much pleased at this, thinking that by this means he would be able to distinguish the men in his kingdom who were legitimate sons of their supposed fathers from those who were not, and so be enabled to increase his treasures, for among the Moors only legitimate children inherit their father's property; and for this end he ordered a palace to be appropriated to the manufacture of this cloth. And these men, in order to convince him that they had no intention of deceiving him, agreed to be shut up in this palace until the cloth was manufactured, which satisfied the King.

"When they were supplied with a large quantity

of gold, silver, silk, and many other things, they
entered the palace, and, putting their looms in
order, gave it to be understood that they were
working all day at the cloth.

"After some days, one of them came to the King
and told him the cloth was commenced, that it was
the most curious thing in the world, describing the
design and construction; he then prayed the King
to favour them with a visit, but begged he would
come alone. The King was much pleased, but
wishing to have the opinion of some one first, sent
the Lord Chamberlain to see it, in order to know if
they were deceiving him. When the Lord Chamberlain saw the workmen, and heard all they had to
say, he dared not admit he could not see the cloth,
and when he returned to the King he stated that he
had seen it; the King sent yet another, who gave
the same report. When they whom he had sent
declared that they had seen the cloth he determined
to go himself.

"On entering the palace and seeing the men at
work, who began to describe the texture and relate
the origin of the invention as also the design and
colour, in which they all appeared to agree, although
in reality they were not working; when the King
saw how they appeared to work, and heard the
character of the cloth so minutely described, and
yet could not see it, although those he had sent had
seen it, he began to feel very uneasy, fearing he
might not be the son of the King, who was sup-

posed to be his father, and that if he acknowledged he could not see the cloth he might lose his kingdom; under this impression he commenced praising the fabric, describing its peculiarities after the manner of the workmen.

"On the return to his palace he related to his people how good and marvellous was the cloth, yet at the same time suspected something wrong.

"At the end of two or three days the King requested his 'Alguacil' (or officer of justice) to go and see the cloth. When the Alguacil entered and saw the workmen, who, as before, described the figures and pattern of the cloth, knowing that the King had been to see it, and yet could not see it himself, he thought he certainly could not be the legitimate son of his father, and therefore could not see it. He, however, feared if he was to declare that he could not see it he would lose his honourable position; to avoid this mischance he commenced praising the cloth even more vehemently than the others.

"When the Alguacil returned to the King and told him that he had seen the cloth, and that it was the most extraordinary production in the world, the King was much disconcerted; for he thought that if the Alguacil had seen the cloth, which he was unable to see, there could no longer be a doubt that he was not the legitimate son of the King, as was generally supposed, he therefore did not hesitate to praise the excellency of the cloth and the skill of the workmen who were able to make it.

ᶦ "On another day he sent one of his Councillors,
and it happened to him as to the King and the
others of whom I have spoken; and in this manner
and for this reason they deceived the King and
many others, for no one dared to say he could not
see the cloth.

"Things went on thus until there came a great
feast, when all requested the King to be dressed in
some of the cloth; so the workmen, being ordered,
brought some rolled up in a very fine linen and inquired of the King how much of it he wished them
to cut off; so the King gave orders how much and
how to make it up.

" Now when the clothes were made and the feast
day had arrived the weavers brought them to the
King, informing his Majesty that his dress was made
of the cloth as he had directed, the King all this
time not daring to say he could not see it.

"When the King had professed to dress himself
in this suit he mounted on horseback and rode into
the city; but fortunately for him it was summer
time. The people seeing his Majesty come in this
manner were much surprised; but knowing that
those who could not see this cloth would be considered illegitimate sons of their fathers, kept their
surprise to themselves, fearing the dishonour consequent upon such a declaration. Not so, however,
with a negro, who happened to notice the King
thus equipped; for he, having nothing to lose, came
to him and said, ' Sire, to me it matters not whose

son I am, therefore I tell you that you are riding without any clothes.' On this the King commenced beating him, saying that he was not the legitimate son of his supposed father, and therefore it was that he could not see the cloth. But no sooner had the negro said this, than others were convinced of its truth, and said the same; until, at last, the King and all with him lost their fear of declaring the truth, and saw through the trick of which these impostors had made them the victims. When the weavers were sought for they were found to have fled, taking with them all they had received from the King by their imposition.

"Now you, Count Lucanor, since that man of whom you speak forbids your trusting to any one, and demands your entire confidence, be careful you are not deceived; for, you ought to know very well that he can have no reason for seeking your advantage more than his own; nor has he more reason to serve you than have those who are indebted to you and are already in your service."

Count Lucanor found this to be good advice, so adopted it.

And Don Juan, also seeing that it was a good example, wrote it in this book and made these lines, which say as follows:—

> Who counsels thee to secrecy with friends
> Seeks to entrap thee for his own base ends,

NOTE.

This story, so quaintly and graphically written, stands alone in the interest of its details, neither the *Short Mantle*, which figures under the title of the "Manteau mal taillé," in the *Fabliaux* of the thirteenth century, nor the "Enchanted Bowl" of Ariosto, nor indeed any of the romance writers of that age contain any subject wherein the various passions and interests which move mankind are so well delineated.

The false promises made by the impostors, arising out of want and desperation, recall to mind the old Spanish proverb, "Cuando el Corsario promete misas y cera, con mal anda la galera; (The galley is in a bad way when the Corsair promises masses and candles)."

CHAPTER VIII.

What happened to a King with a man who called himself an Alchymist.

ONE day Count Lucanor conversed with Patronio in the following manner :—

"Patronio, a man came and told me he possessed a secret which would enable me to acquire great riches and honour, but that to begin the work certain sums of money would be required; and this being furnished, he promised to return me tenfold on my outlay. Now, since God has blessed you with a good understanding, tell me what you think most desirable to be done under such circumstances."

"My lord," said Patronio, "in order that you
may know how to act, having regard for your own
interest, under such circumstances, I should like to
inform you what happened to a king with a man
who called himself an alchymist."

The Count desired him to relate it.

"There was once," said he, "a man who being a
great adventurer desired by some means or other to
enrich himself and rise out of the miserable situation
in which he then was. Knowing of a certain King
who taxed his people heavily, and was very anxious
to acquire a knowledge of alchymy, he procured a
hundred doublas * 'and filed them down, mixing the
gold dust so procured with other metals, and from
this alloy he made a hundred false coins, each
weighing as much as a doubla. He then took a
supply of these spurious coins, dressed himself as a
quiet and respectable man, and went to the city
where the King dwelt, and, entering the shop of a
grocer, sold to him the whole of his counterfeits for
about two or three doublas. The purchaser inquired
the name and use of these coins, to which he replied,
'They are essential to the practice of alchymy, and
are called *tabardit.*'

"Now, our adventurer continued to reside in this
city for some time as a respectable and well-dressed
man, and it became circulated as a secret that he
knew the science of alchymy. When this news

* An ancient Spanish gold coin.

reached the King, he sent for him and asked if he
were an alchymist.

"He, however, appeared as if anxious to conceal
his knowledge, and replied that he was not, but
ultimately admitted that he was, at the same time
telling the King that no man but himself knew the
secret, and that no great outlay was required; but
that, if his Majesty desired it, he could furnish him
with a little of the ingredients, and then show him
all he knew of the science. This pleased the King
very much, as it appeared, according to the alchymist's
representation, that he would incur no risk. Our
adventurer now sends, in the King's name, for the
things required, among them being the *tabardit*,
which were easily procured at a cost of not more
than three dineros,* and when they were brought
and melted down before the King there was produced the weight of a doubla of fine gold. The
King, seeing that these materials which cost so little
produced a doubla, was delighted, and told the
alchymist that he considered him to be a most
worthy man, giving him an order to make more.

"Our adventurer replied, as if he had no more
information to give, 'Sire, all that I know I have
shown to you, and henceforth you will be able to do
it as well as myself. Nevertheless, should any of
the ingredients be wanting, it will be quite impossible
to produce gold.' Saying this, he departed for his
own house.

* An ancient Spanish copper coin.

"The King now procured some of the materials himself, and made gold; he then doubled the quantity and produced the weight of two doublas; again doubling this quantity, he produced four doublas of gold; and so, in proportion, as he increased the weight of the ingredients, he produced an increase of gold. When the King saw that he could make any quantity of gold he desired, he ordered as much of the material to be brought him as would produce a thousand doublas. So the quantity was brought him as he desired, with the exception of the *tabardit* which could not be got. The King, seeing that the *tabardit* was wanting, and that without it he could not make gold, sent for the alchymist and told him he was unable to make gold as he had been accustomed to do.

"On this the alchymist begged to know if he had all the ingredients the same as hitherto.

"The King replied, 'Yes, all except the *tabardit*.'

"'Then,' said the alchymist, 'although you have all the other things, yet, failing this one, you cannot, as I told you at first, expect to make gold.'

The King then asked if he knew where to procure the *tabardit*, and he was answered in the affirmative; the King then requested that he should procure for him a sufficient quantity to make as much gold as he might desire.

"The alchymist now replied that any other person could obtain it as well as himself, and, perhaps, better; but, if the King particularly wished it, he would return for some to his own country, where he could procure any amount. The King then counted and found that, including all expenses, it would cost a large sum to procure this one ingredient, but he furnished our adventurer with the sum required and sent him on this service.

"As soon as the alchymist had received the money he went away in great haste, never to return.

"When the King found that the alchymist remained away longer than he ought, he sent his servants to his house to know if there had been any tidings of him, but they found none whatever; but at his house was left a small chest which was locked; this they opened, and in it they found a paper on which was written, 'I know well there is no such thing in the world as *tabardit*, but be assured that your Majesty has been deceived. When I came to you and said that I could enrich you, you ought to have said to me, " First enrich thyself, and then I will believe thee." '

"Some days after this, some men were laughing and amusing themselves by writing the names and characters of their friends and acquaintances, saying, such and such were intelligent, such and such were foolish, and of others in like manner, good and bad. Amongst those classed as imprudent was found the name of the King. When the King heard of it, he sent for the authors of this writing, and, having assured them that no harm should come to them, demanded why they had placed his name amongst those of imprudent men. They then answered him, 'Because you have entrusted so much treasure to a stranger of whom you had not the least knowledge.'

"The King replied that they were mistaken, for should the man return he would bring with him much gold.

"'Then,' said they, 'our opinion would lose nothing; for, should he return, we will erase your name and insert his.'

"And you, Count Lucanor, if you do not wish to be considered a man of weak understanding, must not risk so much of your property for a thing that is uncertain; otherwise, you may have to repent sacrificing the certain for the uncertain."

This advice pleased the Count much, so he acted upon it, and found the result good.

And Don Juan, seeing this to be a good example, ordered it to be written in this book, with these following lines :—

> To venture much of thy wealth refuse
> On the faith of a man who has nought to lose.

NOTE.

This tale, so full of point and humour, is, as we see in the paper found in the alchymist's trunk, not without its bearing on the caution required in daily life, to avoid impositions; as, also, the dangers to which cupidity exposes men who grasp at every delusive project to gratify their passion for gain.

It may be, also, that Don Manuel desired in this narrative to ridicule the follies of alchymy, to which his learned uncle, Alfonso X, was much addicted, and the belief in which was so universal in the middle ages.

CHAPTER IX.

Of that which happened to two Cavaliers who were in the service of the Infant Prince Henry.

OUNT LUCANOR, conversing one day with his friend Patronio, addressed him in the following manner :—

"Patronio, for a long time I have had an enemy who has done me much injury; nor can I say that I have not done the same to him—in fact, we live in a state of constant warfare with each other. And now it happens that another man, much more powerful than either of us, is about to commence a war against him and me; and this man is in a position to do us both a serious injury. Seeing this to be the case, my old enemy comes to me to say that we should lose no time in defending ourselves against this our common foe; for that, if both unite against him, it is certain that we shall be safe: but, if one keeps apart from the other, it is equally certain that whichever of us he might first select would easily be conquered by him; and, that one being vanquished, he who remained would become an easy victim. So, you see, Patronio, that I am in great perplexity as to how I shall act. On both sides I have much to fear; my former enemy is not wanting in will to injure me, and, should he at any time find me in his power, I am not sure of my life. Whatever arrangement we may make, I shall feel no confidence in him, or he in me; and these considerations keep me in perpetual anxiety. On the other hand, as you you will perceive, if we are not friends, as he wishes, we shall both be seriously injured. Now, as I have great confidence in your abilities, I pray you to advise me how to act under such circumstances."

"My lord," said Patronio, "your position is very critical and not without danger. In order that you may better understand how to act, it is desirable that you should know what happened at Tunis to two cavaliers who lived with the Infant Prince Henry."

The Count desired to be informed, and Patronio proceeded :—

"Two cavaliers who were in the service of the Infant, at Tunis, were such excellent friends that they resided together in the same house. Each had his own horse; and, in proportion as these friends loved each other, so did their horses appear to detest each other. Now, these cavaliers were not rich, and consequently, were unable to maintain separate establishments; but, owing to the viciousness of their horses, they found it impossible to reside any longer together, so very reluctantly separated. Things had gone on in this way for some time, when, finding nothing could be done to remedy the evil, they spoke to the Infant concerning it, and begged he would give their horses to a lion

5

which was kept by the King of Tunis. The Infant complied with their request, and spoke to the King, telling him how the cavaliers were annoyed by the viciousness of their horses, and asking the King's permission to have these horses turned into the lion's court.

" When the two vicious horses found themselves loose in the lion's court, but before the lion had sallied forth from his den, they commenced kicking and biting more violently than ever. While they were so fighting, the door of the lion's den, leading into the court, was thrown open.

" As soon as the two horses saw the lion leave his den for the court they began to tremble violently, and by degrees approached each other till they were so close together as to appear almost one. They then conjointly attacked the lion, kicking and biting him so furiously that he was compelled to retreat into the den from whence he came.

" From this time the two horses continued good friends. They ate together from the same crib, and lived together in a very small stable.

" Thus, you see, my lord, from the great and common terror these two vicious horses had of the lion arose a lasting friendship. And you, Count Lucanor, if you believe that your old enemy fears so much his and your common enemy, and requires your assistance so urgently as to induce him to forget the feuds which have hitherto existed between you, knowing that he cannot defend himself without your assistance, then I hold that, like the two horses, it will be advisable that you approach each other by degrees until you have so united your forces as to lose all fear and distrust of each other. But, mark you ! until you acquire this necessary confidence in your ally, you must proceed with a certain amount of caution. If you find him acting at all times with good faith and loyalty, and know for certain that he has no intention to revenge himself on you, or do any injury to you, then it will be better that you unite with him in earnest, in order that the stranger may not conquer or destroy you; for it is even better to suffer the ills you now complain of than those of your new enemy, the extent of which you cannot foresee; but, should anything occur to give you reason for doubting the sincerity of your ally, then it would be wrong to assist him, for he might lead you into great peril to secure his own safety. It remains, therefore, that you be vigilant, whilst preparing to guard against the combined danger threatened you by a new adversary and your former enemy."

"Count Lucanor was much pleased with what Patronio had related, and found that he had given him very good advice. Also Don Juan thought this a very good example, so he commanded it to be written in this book, and wrote these lines, which say thus :—

When danger threatens, enemies unite,
And join, as friends, to carry on the fight.

NOTES TO CHAPTER IX.

The Infant Prince Henry mentioned in this chapter was the son of Ferdinand III. (called the Saint), and his queen, Beatrice. Being persecuted by his brother, Alfonso X, after many dangers, sought refuge in Tunis, about the year 1259. The Bey, knowing his rank, and admiring his courage, gave him, after a time, the entire command of his army; a position he held for a period of four years, during which time he became renowned for many acts of valour, so that many Castilians sought for appointments in the army under his command, and fought with him under the flag of Tunis. Of these were the two cavaliers spoken of in this narrative. The Moors of the court, becoming jealous of the position held by the prince, conspired to impress the Bey with the notion that there existed a plot to murder him and place the Infant on the throne. Hearing this, the king became alarmed, and, judging any means of escape justifiable, made an appointment with the Infant for a secret conference, which, being punctually kept by the un-suspecting prince, he found himself face to face with the lions of the Bey. The prince, seeing the peril of his position, drew his sword and awaited the attack. Happily, however, the animals remained immovable and allowed him to retire uninjured. The Bey, frustrated in his design, and ashamed of his intentions, ordered the Infant to immediately leave his territories, together with all the Christians: which was done, resistance being impossible. After an adventurous life, this hero returned to Spain on the death of his nephew, Sancho the Brave, and he there forced the people to name him tutor to Ferdinand IV, and died in 1304. This history is interesting in so far that it leads us to the source from whence Don Manuel has doubtless derived the relation given in his narrative. The Infant Henry, to whom this affair in Tunis happened, being his uncle, it may be that the circumstance as related did actually occur to the two cavaliers of his retinue.

CHAPTER X.

Concerning what happened to a Seneschal. of Carcasona.

ANOTHER time, when Count Lucanor was conversing with Patronio, he spoke to him in the following manner :—

"Patronio, as I know that death is unavoidable, I would now, while I have yet time, found some work of charity which may hereafter be applied for the benefit of my soul, and of which good act all the world may be cognizant. I pray you, therefore, to advise me how best to accomplish this end.'

"My lord," said Patronio, "whatever you do, whatever may be your object, or whatever your intentions, act always with honour and justice. But, as you desire to know how a man should act so as to benefit his soul and increase his reputation, I should be much pleased by being permitted to relate to you what happened to a Seneschal of Carcasona."

The Count desired to be informed what that was.

"My lord, a Seneschal of Carcasona being seriously ill, and informed that he was not likely to recover, sent for the Prior of the Dominican Friars

and the Guardian of the Franciscan Order, and
informed them what he wished they should do for
the salvation of his soul, and desired that if he died
they would see fulfilled all the dispositions of his
will.   They, on their part, willingly agreed, for he
left much for alms, prayers, and masses. Now, when
all his charitable dispositions had been complied
with, the friars were well satisfied, and hoped trust-
ingly for the eternal salvation of his soul.

"It happened some short time after this that there
was a woman in the town said to be possessed of
the Devil, and who spoke most extraordinary things.
The friars, hearing this, thought it advisable to go
to her and inquire if she knew anything respecting
the soul of the Seneschal, and they did so.

"As soon as they entered the house where the
possessed woman lived, and before they could put
any questions to her, she cried out, that she well
knew why they were come, and that the soul of the
Seneschal was in hell, where she had left it a short
time ago.

"When the friars heard this, they told her she
lied, for they were certain that the Seneschal had
humbly confessed and devoutly received the sacra-
ments of the holy Mother Church; and that, since
the Christian faith was infallible, it was not possible ·
that what she said could be true.

"She replied, that, without doubt, the faith and
law of Christians are very true, but that he had not
acted as a sincere Christian before his death; that,

however much he might have given, hoping thus to
secure the salvation of his soul, still it was not given
with a good grace—for he had commanded that the
charitable dispositions of his will should only be
executed in case he died, when he could no longer
retain possession of his riches nor carry them with
him to the grave. Had he recovered, he never
intended fulfilling any part of these charitable intentions. Moreover, he regarded only the opinion of
those around him and of the world, hoping thus to
obtain fame and honour by his charitable donations.
Therefore, although he did a good act, it was not
well done, since man must be judged by his intentions ; and the intentions of the Seneschal were
not good, although they may have appeared so;
therefore he has received his reward.

"And you, Count Lucanor, since you desire my
counsel, I give you that which appears to me most
valuable. It is, if you wish to do good, to do it
while you have life, if you hope for a reward hereafter. The first thing required of you is to repair
the wrongs you may have done, for little will it
avail you to steal the sheep and offer the feet to
God. So, likewise, you will benefit little by holding
the fruit of robbery and spoliation, although you
may give alms out of your ill-gotten gains. In order
that your alms may be worthy of acceptance, it is
necessary that they partake of the following conditions :—firstly, that the gift be a part of your own
rightful property, given under the influence of a true

and contrite spirit, not from the superfluities, but from that which the giver is in need of himself Again, the donation should be made during life; and, lastly, it should be done simply for the love of God, and not through vain-glory or worldly feeling. The fulfilling these conditions constitutes righteous almsgiving, for which a man may expect to be well rewarded. Nevertheless, neither you nor any one else should fail to do good, although they may not be able to fulfil all the above conditions; that would be very weak and unwise, for certain it is that a good action always claims its reward. Meritorious works draw men from sin, induce to repentance, and to the well-being of the soul, tending even to fame and worldly advantages. All good actions tend to good; nevertheless, they will be more available for salvation and more profitable to his soul if a man act under the influence of the conditions above mentioned."

And Count Lucanor, considering what Patronio said was true, resolved to follow his advice, and prayed to God for grace to enable him to do so.

And Don Juan, finding that this was a very good example, caused it to be written in this book, and made these lines, which say :—

> In aim, as well as deed, be pure,
> If you would make your glory sure.

NOTES.

The lesson taught in this tale was a severe one for the superior clergy, who were at this period not noted for their humility or abnegation; as it was also a reflection upon the tenacity of some men, not only to life, but to life's treasures, by the illustration of an attempt to cheat Providence into the salvation of his soul, by giving what the dying man could no longer retain. It reminds us of the Spanish anecdote, where a dying bequest records that "if the missing cow was found it should be for the children; if not, it should be for God." The same nation has also a saying referring to the Abbot of Bamba, on spurious benevolence. "El Abad de Bamba lo que no poede comer lo da por su Alma."—"*The Abbot of Bamba gives away for the good of his soul that which he cannot eat.*"

In his fable of The Sick Man and the Angel, Gay has powerfully illustrated the moral conveyed by Don Manuel in this history— the futility of the hope that heaven may be purchased by a posthumous legacy for pious uses of the wealth that has been hoarded during life for selfish purposes.

CHAPTER XI.

Of that which happened to a Moor who had a Sister pretending to be alarmed at any ordinary occurrence.

ANOTHER day, Count Lucanor, conversing with his friend Patronio, said, "Patronio, you know that I have an elder brother. We are sons of the same parents, and, because of his seniority, I look

on him as if he were my father; and, as such, he
expects me to obey him. He passes for a good
Christian and has credit for being prudent, but it
has pleased God that I should be richer and more
powerful than he is; and, although he is careful to
disguise the feeling, yet I am certain he is jealous
of me. Whenever I need his assistance, or require
anything from him, he gives me to understand that
he cannot help me, because it would be sinful, and
always breaks off the affair by excusing himself in
this manner; while at other times, when he requires
my assistance, he tells me it is incumbent on me to
serve him, although, in doing so, I might lose everything in this world; in fact, he says I ought not to
hesitate in' risking even my life in his service—and
all this to oblige him only. Under such circumstances, I pray you to advise me how to act, and
what is my real duty."

" My lord," said Patronio, "it appears to me that
your brother's actions, to say the least of them, are
selfish, and much resemble those of the sister of a
certain Moor, which I would relate to you."

The Count desired him to do so.

" My lord, a Moor had an over-indulged sister,
who prided herself in appearing timid; and to such
an extent did she carry this whim that she feigned
alarm at the most ordinary occurrence, even when
she drank water out of one of the narrow-necked
earthen jars (such as were then generally used), and
heard the water gurgling as it flowed, she pretended

to be very much afraid of it. The Moor, being informed of this, was much annoyed. Now the brother was a fine young man, but very poor, and was compelled by necessity to follow a most disgraceful way of obtaining a living. Poverty often compels a man to do that of which he would otherwise feel ashamed, and such was the case with the Moor, who did thus : when he heard of any rich person being buried, he would go by night to the tomb, disinter the body, and strip it of its shroud and all else of value ; and, by the sale of these articles, he maintained himself and his sister, she, all the time, knowing that her brother supported her by the proceeds of this sacrilege.

"Now it happened about this time that a rich man died, and was interred in very valuable clothes and other costly things. When the sister knew of this, she told her brother that she would assist him that night in taking away the valuables from the rich man's tomb.

"When night came, the young man and his sister repaired to the tomb containing the corpse, and opened it ; and, when they had helped themselves to all that was worth taking, they found that the clothes could not be removed without tearing unless they broke the neck of the corpse. The sister, seeing that this would deprive them of much of their value, took the head in her hands, and, without evincing any feeling or pity, broke the neck and drew away the clothes. They then, with their booty, returned home.

"Some little time after this, when they were sitting at table, the sister drank out of the water-jar, and again hearing the gurgling sound feigned alarm and declared that she should faint.   Upon this the brother, remembering that without fear she had broken the neck of the dead man, said, in Arabic, '*A ha ya! hati, tassa niboa valo tassa ni fortuheni;*' that is to say, 'Ha, ha! sister, you fear then the sound of the water-jar, which says, "batu, batu," but were not afraid to break the neck of a dead man.'   And this saying is even till this day a proverb amongst the Moors.

"And I should say, my lord, that your elder brother, if he excuses himself in the selfish, unjust, manner you have described, resembles, in a great measure, the sister of the Moor.

" Now, for the future, should your brother demand your assistance, in return giving you only fine words and excuses, do not retaliate, but, more than this, do all that he requires of you, taking care that you do not fall into sin, nor act against your conscience or interest by so doing."

The Count considered this advice to be good, and, acting accordingly, found it to answer well.

And Don Juan, being of opinion that this was a good example, caused it to be written in this book, and made these lines, which say as follows :—

> He who declines to help thee in thy need,
> For aid himself in vain one day may plead.

NOTE.

This is not one of the author's happiest productions, in so far, however, only, that the narrative does not illustrate (as it evidently was intended to do) the moral it purports to convey. Legrand D'Aussy has given a very free imitation of this tale under the title of "The young Lady who could never hear a certain exclamation without fainting,"—"De la Demoiselle qui ne pouvait, sans se pâmer, entendre un certain jurement." We find another version of it in the Collection of Berbazan.

CHAPTER XII.

Of that which happened to a Dean of Santiago, with Don Illan, the Magician, who lived at Toledo.

ONE day Count Lucanor was conversing with Patronio, whose advice he sought under the following circumstances. "Patronio," said he, "a man came to me and begged I would assist him, knowing I was able to do so, promising to serve me in return, at any time, either for the promotion of my interest or honour. I rendered him all the assistance in my power, when, before his trouble was removed (although he believed it to be so), a circumstance happened in which I knew he could render me assistance, which I begged him to do; but he made me some excuse. Since then another case has arisen where he could have been of service to me, but again, as before, he has excused himself, and in every instance when I have needed his help he has always declined assisting me under some plea or other. Now his difficulties are not yet removed, nor can they be without my assistance. I, therefore, pray you, having so much confidence in your judgment, to advise me how to act under such circumstances."

"Count Lucanor," said Patronio, "in order that you may know how to act in such a case, it is desirable that you should hear what happened to a Dean of Santiago, with Don Illan, who was a great magician, and dwelt in Toledo."

The Count begged he would narrate it.

"My lord," said Patronio, "there was a Dean of Santiago who had a great desire to be initiated in the art of necromancy; and, hearing that Don Illan of Toledo knew more of this art than any other person in that country, came to Toledo with a view of studying under him. On the day of his arrival he proceeded to the house of Don Illan, whom he found reading in a retired chamber, and who received him very graciously, desiring him not to inform him of the motive of his visit until he had first partaken of his repast, which was found excellent, and consisted of every delicacy that could be desired.

"Now, when the repast was concluded, the dean

took the magician aside and told him the motive
of his visit, urging him very earnestly to instruct
him in the art in which he was so great an adept,
and which he, the dean, desired so anxiously to be
made acquainted with.

"When Don Illan told him that he was a dean
and, consequently, a man of great influence, and
that he would attain a high position, saying, at the
same time, that men, generally speaking, when
they reach an elevated position and attain the
objects of their ambition, forget easily what others
have previously done for them, as also all past obligations and those from whom they received them—
failing generally in the performance of their former
promises, the dean assured him such should not
be the case with him; saying, no matter to what
eminence he might attain, he would not fail to do
everything in his power to help his former friends,
and the magician in particular.

"In this way they conversed until supper-time
approached; and now, the covenant between them
being completed, Don Illan said to the dean, that, in
teaching him the art he desired to learn, it would be
necessary for them to retire to some distant apartment, and, taking him by the hand, led him to a
chamber. As they were quitting the dining-room,
he called his housekeeper, desiring her to procure
some partridges for their supper that night, but not
to cook them until she had his special commands.
Having said this, he sought the dean and conducted

him to the entrance of a beautifully carved stone
staircase, by which they descended a considerable
distance, appearing as if they had passed under the
river Tagus, and, arriving at the bottom of the steps,
they found a suite of rooms and a very elegant
chamber, where were arranged the books and instruments of study ; and, having here seated themselves,
they were debating which should be the first books
to read, when two men entered by the door and
gave the dean a letter which had been sent to him
by his uncle the archbishop, informing him that he
was dangerously ill, and that if he wished to see him
alive it would be requisite for him to come immediately. The dean was much moved by this news
—partly on account of the illness of his uncle, but
more through the fear of being obliged to abandon
his favourite study, just commenced—so he wrote
a respectful letter to his uncle the archbishop, which
he sent by the same messengers. At the end of four
days, other men arrived on foot bringing fresh letters
to the dean, informing him that the archbishop was
dead, and that all those interested in the welfare of
the Church were desirous that he should succeed to
his late uncle's dignity, telling him, at the same time,
it was quite unnecessary for him to inconvenience
himself by returning immediately, as his nomination
would be better secured were he not present in the
church. At the end of seven or eight days, two
squires arrived, very richly dressed and accoutred,
who, after kissing his hand, delivered to him the

letters informing him that he had been appointed archbishop.

"When Don Illan heard this he told him he was much pleased that this good news had arrived during his stay in his house ; and, as God had been so gracious to him, begged that the deanery now vacant might be given to his son.

"The archbishop elect replied, that he hoped Don Illan would allow him to name to the vacancy his own brother, saying, at the same time, that he would present him with some office in his own church with which his son would be contented, inviting, at the same time, both father and son to accompany him to Santiago.

"To this they consented ; and all three departed for the city, where they were received with much honour. After they had resided there some time, there arrived one day messengers from the Pope bearing letters naming the former dean Bishop of Tolosa, permitting him at the same time to name whom he pleased to succeed him in his vacant see.

"When Don Illan heard this he reminded him of his promise, urging him to confer the appointment on his son. But the archbishop again desired that he would allow him to name one of his paternal uncles to succeed him. Don Illan replied, that, although he felt he was unjustly treated, still, relying on the future accomplishment of his promise, he should let it be. The archbishop thanked him again renewed his promise of future services and,

6

inviting Don Illan and his son to accompany him, they all set out for Tolosa, where they were well received by the counts and great men of the country.

"They had resided there about two years when messengers again came from the Pope with letters in which he announced to the archbishop that he had named him cardinal, allowing him, as before, to name his successor.

"On this occasion Don Illan went to him, and again urging that many vacancies had taken place, to none of which he had named his son, so that now he could plead no excuse, and he hoped the cardinal would confer this last dignity on his son. But once more the cardinal requested Don Illan would forgive his having bestowed the vacant see on one of his maternal uncles; saying he was a very good old man, and proposing they should now depart for Rome, where undoubtedly he would do for them all they could desire. Don Illan complained very much; nevertheless, he consented to accompany the cardinal to Rome. On their arrival they were very well received by the other cardinals and the entire court, and they lived there a long time. Don Illan daily importuned the cardinal to confer some appointment on his son, but he always found some excuse for not doing so.

"While they were yet at Rome, the pope died, and all the cardinals assembled in conclave elected our cardinal pope.

"Then Don Illan came to him, saying, 'You have

now no excuse to offer for not fulfilling the promises you have hitherto made me.'

" But the new pope told him not to importune
him so much, as there was still time to think of him
and his son.

" Don Illan now began to complain in earnest.
' You have,' said he, ' made me very many promises, not one of which you have performed.' He
then recalled to his mind how earnestly he had
pledged his word at their first interview to do all he
could to help him, and never as yet had he done
anything. 'I have no longer any faith in your
words,' said Don Illan, ' nor do I now expect anything from you.'

" These expressions very much angered the pope,
who replied, tartly, ' If I am again annoyed in this
manner I will have you thrown into prison as a
heretic and a sorcerer, for I know well that in
Toledo, where you lived, you had no other means
of support but by practising the art of necromancy.'

" When Don Illan saw how ill the pope had re-
quited him for what he had done, he prepared to
depart, the pope refusing to grant him wherewith
to support himself on the road. ' Then,' said he to
the pope, ' since I have nothing to eat, I must needs
fall back upon the partridges I ordered for to-night's
supper.' He then called out to his housekeeper, and
ordered her to cook the birds for his supper.

" No sooner had he spoken, than the dean found
himself again in Toledo, still dean of Santiago, as

on his arrival, but so overwhelmed with shame that
he knew not what to say.

"'How fortunate is it,' said Don Illan to him,
'that I have thus proved the intrinsic value of your
promises in prosperity; for, as it is, I should have
considered it a great misfortune had I allowed you
to partake of the partridges.'

"And you, Count Lucanor, will now see how
you ought to act towards the man, who, desiring
your assistance, is so ungrateful. Risk not too much
on the chance of your services being repaid at some
future time, or you may anticipate the reward Don
Illan received from the dean.'

The Count found this to be very good advice,
acted upon it, and was benefited.

And Don Juan, thinking this to be a very good
example, had it written in this book and composed
these verses, which say as follows :—

> Who pays thy kindness with ungratefulness,
> The more he has to give, he'll give the less.

NOTE.

Under the title of the "Dean of Badajoz," Herder, and,
after him, L'Abbé Blanchet, have given another version,
which has furnished Andrieux with the subject of one of his
prettiest tales in verse. The editor of Blanchet's works says,
"This is not an oriental tale, but is taken from El Conde Lucanor, a highly esteemed Spanish work of the fourteenth century, written by the Infant Don Manuel." The Abbé, however, has so interlarded the original story with adornments of
his own, bearing critically on the ecclesiastical condition of his
time, that it would be difficult for Don Manuel to recognize
his own tale in its French dress.

85

CHAPTER XIII.

*What happened to King Ben Abit, of Seville, with
Queen Romaquia his wife.*

THE Count conversed with Patronio one
day in the following manner :—

"There is a man," said he, " who
has begged me frequently to assist him,
and, whenever I have done so, he has always given
me to understand how grateful he feels. Lately, he
has again called upon me for aid, but I find if I do
not do as he requires, he becomes angry, and does
not fail to give me to understand, by his manner,
that he has forgotten all his previous obligations.
Now, as you are a man of good understanding, I
beg you advise me how I should act towards this
man."

"Count Lucanor," said Patronio, "it appears to
me that what has occurred to you with this man
resembles much that which happened to the King
Ben Abit, of Seville, with the Queen Romaquia, his
wife."

The Count begged him to recount what that
was.

"My lord," said Patronio, "the King Abit, of
Seville, was married to Romaquia, and he loved

her better than anything in the world. She was a very virtuous woman, and the Moors recount many of her good acts.   But in one thing she did not display much wisdom; this was, that she generally had some caprice or other which the king was always willing to gratify.

"One day, being in Cordova during the month of February, there happened to be (which was very unusual) a very heavy fall of snow. When Romaquia saw this she began to weep. The king, seeing her so afflicted, desired to know the cause of her grief.

"'I weep,' said she, 'because I am not permitted to live in a country where we sometimes see snow.'

The king, anxious to gratify her, ordered almond trees to be planted on all the mountains surrounding Cordova, for, it being a very warm climate, snow is seldom or never seen there. But now, once a year, and that in the month of February, the almond trees came forth in full blossom, which, from their whiteness, made it appear as if there had been a fall of snow on the mountains, and was a source of great delight to the queen for a time.

"On another occasion, Romaquia being in her apartment, which overlooked the river, saw a woman without shoes or stockings kneading mud on the banks of the river for the purpose of making bricks. When Romaquia saw this she began to cry, which the king observing, begged to know the cause of her grief.

" She replied, ' It is because I am not free to do as I please; I cannot do as yonder woman is doing.'

" Then the king, in order to gratify her, ordered a lake at Cordova to be filled with rose-water in place of ordinary water; and, to produce mud, he had this filled with sugar, powdered cinnamon, and ginger, beautiful stones, amber, musk, and as many other fragrant spices and perfumes as could be procured; and, in place of straws, he ordered to be placed ready small sugar canes. Now when this lake was full of such mud, as you may imagine, the king informed Romaquia that now she might take off her shoes and stockings and enjoy herself by making as many bricks as she pleased.

" Another day, taking a fancy for something not immediately procurable, she began weeping as before. The king again entreated to know the cause of her grief.

" ' How can I refrain from tears,' said she, ' when you never do anything to please me ? '

" The king, seeing that so much had been done to please and gratify her caprices, and feeling now at his wit's end, exclaimed, in Arabic, ' *Ehu alenahac aten,*' which means, ' Not even the day of the mud. That is to say, that, although all the rest had been forgotten, she might at least have remembered the mud he had prepared to humour her.

"And you, Count Lucanor, if you see, after having done so much for this man, that he is ungrateful, and forgets all previous obligations because you are not disposed to do more, I would now advise you to have nothing more to do with him, for he might act in a manner injurious to you.

"But, above all things, I counsel you never to forget a previous obligation, although the person who was once your friend, and conferred it, is no longer disposed to do all you may require."

And the Count thought this very good advice, and, acting upon it, found the results favourable.

And Don Juan, considering it a very good example, caused it to be written in this book, and composed the following lines, which say :—

> Waste not your kindness on one
> Who heeds not the good you have done.

NOTE.

The act of ingenious gallantry recounted in the above chapter is recorded by Condé, author of the "History of the Domination of the Arabs in Spain," as due to Abd el Rahman III, King of Cordova, who reigned from the year 912 to 964; and who, to satisfy the caprice of his queen, or, as is rather supposed, of his mistress Azahra (the flower), caused, as the little history of Don Manuel tells us, the distant mountains to be covered with almond trees; but which, one would. be rather inclined to believe were orange, the flowers of which bear, in Arabic, the same name as that given to the favourite—Azahra. It was for this capricious lady also that the king caused to be built the famous palace of Azahra, near Cordova.

CHAPTER XIV.

Concerning what happened to a Lombardian in Bologna.

OUNT LUCANOR held converse one day with his counsellor, Patronio, in the following manner :—

"Patronio," said the Count, "some men have advised me to enrich myself as much as possible, assuring me it will be more advantageous than anything else, enabling me to meet all contingencies. I pray you, therefore, to tell me what you think of this advice."

"My lord," said Patronio, "it is requisite that great men like yourself should have some riches for many reasons, especially that they may not, through want, leave undone that which they ought to do. But do not understand that these riches should be collected for the mere pleasure of accumulation, while you leave unfulfilled the duties which you owe to your people, or the protection of your honours and estates. For, were you to do so, that which happened to a Lombardian, in Bologna, might happen to you."

"How was that ?" said the Count, requesting him to relate the particulars.

" My lord," said Patronio, " there lived in Bologna
a Lombardian, who had amassed a large fortune,
but had never concerned himself as to the means
therein employed, keeping in view only the accumulation of his riches.   The Lombardian being seized
with a mortal illness, one of his friends, seeing
him in great danger, advised him to confess to Saint
Dominic, who happened to be then in Bologna ; to
which the sick man consented.   When Saint Dominic
was sent for, he desired that a friar should attend
the dying man in his place.   The sons of the
Lombardian, hearing that Saint Dominic had been
sent for, were much concerned, fearing that Saint
Dominic would influence their father to leave all
his possessions for the salvation of his soul, and
that nothing would remain for them.   When the
friar arrived, they told him their father was in a
critical perspiration, and that as soon as it was over
they would inform him of it.   Soon after this, however, the Lombardian lost the use of his speech and
died, nothing necessary having been done for the
salvation of his soul.

" When the day of interment arrived, Saint Dominic was requested to preach his funeral oration.
To this the Saint consented.   In his sermon, referring to the deceased, he quoted from the Gospel as
follows :—*Ubi est thesaurus tuus, ibi est cor tuum,*'
that is to say, ' Where thy treasure is, there is thine
heart also ; ' and l aving said this he turned himself
towards the people, and said, ' My friends, in order

to show you that the words of the Evangelist are true, go and seek for the heart of this man, and I tell you you will not find it in his body, but you will find it in his money chest.'

"They then went to search for the heart in the body of the Lombardian, but it was not there. It was found in his strong box, as Saint Dominic had said, full of maggots, and in a most putrid and infectious condition.

"And you, Count Lucanor, if you desire to accumulate riches as you have been advised, be careful of two things—the one, that the means by which they are obtained be honourable; the other, that you do not place your heart too much on the possession of them: never do anything which you ought not to do, or leave undone that which it is incumbent on you to perform, but let your treasure be in good works, in order that you may receive the grace of God and be worthy the esteem of your people."

And the Count was much pleased with the advice which Patronio gave him, and, acting upon it, found it prosper.

And Don Juan, holding that it was a very good example, ordered it to be put in this book, and made these lines, which say as follows :—

The true treasure gain,
And the false disdain.

NOTE.

The tale related in this chapter is as ancient as it is famous. All countries repeat the moral, in some way or other, it has become a proverb. Where do we not hear the expression, "The avaricious man is heartless." The French have a proverb corresponding to the precept of this example :—"Le cœur de l'avare est au fond de sa cassette,"—"The heart of the miser is at the bottom of his money box." What more particularly distinguishes Don Manuel's tale is the moral commentary which concludes it—that all earthly treasures are perishable.

CHAPTER XV.

What Count Fernan Gonzales said to Nuño Lainez.

NE day, Count Lucanor spoke to Patronio, his counsellor, as follows :—

"Patronio, you know that I am no longer a young man, and that, during my life, I have had many troubles. It is my wish now to inform you that I have resolved from henceforth to enjoy myself—follow the chase and avoid all worldly cares and anxieties. And, since I know that you are always able to give me the best advice, I pray you to counsel me as to this determination."

"Count," said Patronio, "what you have said is very sensible, and I should like to be permitted to inform you what the Count Fernan Gonzales once said to Nuño Lainez."

" Tell me, I pray you," said the Count, " what that was."

" My lord," said Patronio, " the Count Fernan Gonzales, who resided at Burgos, had had much trouble in the defence of his possessions; but, there happening to come a period of peace, Nuño Lainez said to him, ' Now let me advise you henceforth not to concern yourself so much with external troubles, but give yourself some ease and enjoyment, and leave your people a little leisure to amuse themselves.'

" ' No one,' said the Count, ' would feel happier to have leisure to enjoy himself and be at rest than I, if I could; but, as you know, I have had wars with the Moors, with the people of Leon, and with the inhabitants of Navarre. However much we may desire to enjoy ourselves, our enemies would lose no time in taking advantage of us; so if we wished to go hunting with our good falcons—riding on comfortable fat mules up and down the fair plains of Arlanza—leaving the country undefended, however agreeable it might be, it would not be wise. It would be said of us as says the ancient proverb—

'The man is dead and gone;
No more his name is known.'

But, if we avoid self-indulgence and work hard to keep ourselves in a proper state of defence, guarding well our honour, they will say of us when we die—

'The man is dead and gone;
But his name and fame live on.'

Now, since all, good and bad, must die, it does not appear to me right, for the mere sake of self-indulgence, to act in such a manner as to sacrifice to pleasure that fame which should be the reward of our good actions, and remain to us long after we are no more.'

"And you, Count Lucanor, since you know that you must die, I would advise you never for the sake of self-indulgence, or for love of pleasure, to neglect those duties, the fulfilment of which, when you die, shall make your name to survive you."

Now the Count was much pleased with what Patronio said, acted upon it, and found it just.

And, as Don Juan considered this a good example, he caused it to be inserted in this book, and composed the following lines :—

If for vice and wanton pleasure our good fame we spend,
Life is given in meagre measure, and we miss the end.

NOTES.

Fernan Gonzales was one of the independent lords or counts of Castile, who, by their power, so long retarded the unity of Spain. His life was similar to that of all the great vassals of the crown—one of perpetual warfare. He began his reign of power 933 and died in 968, according to Mariana; or 970, according to Ferreras. The noble answer given by him, as related in this tale, is not a poetic invention, but an historical fact, and may be found in the general chronicle arranged by order of Alfonso the Wise. This observation is particularly interesting as relating to Fernan Gonzales, as poets and chroniclers have sung his praises, with those of the Cid, Bernardo al Carpio, and San Fernando. As we stated in another place, the count was the hero of a laudatory poem mentioned by Argote de Molina. A work, also written by an Anti-Castilian, entitled, "Defence of Fernan Gonzales, as Sovereign Count of Castile," and which appeared eight centuries after the demise of the count, shows how his memory was revered by the people.

CHAPTER XVI.

Of what happened to Don Rodrigo Melendez de Valdez.

COUNT LUCANOR conversed one day with Patronio his counsellor in the following manner :—

"Patronio," said he, "you know that one of my neighbours and I have had contentions, that he is a man of great influence and much honoured. It now happens that we are both disposed to possess ourselves of a certain town, and it is positive that whoever arrives there first will possess himself of it, and thus it will be entirely lost to the other. You know, also, that all my servants and dependants are ready to march, and I have every reason to believe that, with God's help, if I proceed at once, I shall succeed with great honour and advantage. But there is this impediment; not being in good health, I shall not be able to avail myself of this opportunity. Now I regret much the loss of this town; but I acknowledge to you that to lose it in this manner provokes me still more, as I lose also the honour which the possession of it would give. Having great confidence in your understanding, I pray you tell me what is best to be done."

"My lord," said Patronio, "I can understand your anxiety in this matter; and, in order that you may know how to act always for the best in cases like this, I should be much pleased to relate to you what happened to Don Rodrigo Melendez de Valdez."

The Count desired him to relate what that was.

"Count Lucanor," said Patronio, "Don Rodrigo Melendez de Valdez was a knight much honoured in the kingdom of Leon, and was accustomed, whenever any misfortune happened to him, to exclaim, 'God be praised! for, since he has so willed it, it is for the best.' This Don Rodrigo was counsellor to, and a great favourite with, the King of Leon. He had many enemies, who, through jealousy, reported so many falsehoods, and induced the king to think so ill of him as to order him to be put to death.

"Now, Don Rodrigo, being at his own residence, he received the king's command to attend him. Meanwhile those who were employed to assassinate him waited quietly about half a league from his house. Don Rodrigo intended going on horseback to the king, but, coming down stairs, he fell and broke his leg. When his attendants who were to have accompanied him saw this accident, they were much grieved, but commenced saying, half jocosely, to Don Rodrigo, 'You know you always say, "that which God permits is ever for the best:" now, do you think this is for the best?'

"He replied, that they might be certain, however much this accident was to be deplored, yet he would say to them, since it was by the will of God, it was surely for the best, and all they might say could never change his opinions.

"Now those who were waiting to kill Don Rodrigo by the king's command, when they found he did not come, and knew what had happened to him, returned to the palace to explain why they could not fulfil his orders.

"Don Rodrigo was a long time confined to his house, and unable to mount his horse. During this delay the king ascertained how Don Rodrigo had been calumniated, and, having ordered the slanderers to be seized, went himself to the house of Don Rodrigo Melendez de Valdez, and related to him the slanders that had been propagated against him, and for the fault that he the king, had committed, in ordering him to be put to death, entreated pardon; and, in consideration thereof, bestowed on him new honours and riches. And justice was satisfied by the speedy punishment of those who had reported such falsehoods. In this way God delivered Don Rodrigo, who was not guilty. Hence was his customary affirmation proved true,—that, 'Whatever

7

God permitted to happen was always for the best.'

"And you, Count Lucanor, should not complain of this hindrance to the fulfilment of your wishes. Be certain, in your heart, that 'whatever God wills is for the best;' and, if you will but trust in Him, He will cause all things to work for your good.

"But you ought to understand that these things which happen are of two kinds. The one is when a misfortune happens to a man which admits of no relief: the other is when a misfortune is remediable. Now, when an evil can be cured, it is a man's duty to exert all his energies to obtain the necessary relief, and not remain inactive, saying, 'it is chance, or 'it is the will of God,' for this would be to tempt Providence. But, since man is endowed with under-standing and reason, it is his duty to endeavour to overcome the misfortunes which may befall him, when they will admit of alleviation. But, in those cases where there is no remedy, then man must patiently submit, since it is really the will of God, which is always for the best.

"And as this which has happened to you is clearly one of those afflictions sent by God, and admits of no remedy; and as what God permits is for the best, rest therefore assured that God will so direct circumstances that the result will be as you desire."

And the Count held that Patronio had spoken wisely, and that it was good advice; and, acting accordingly, he found good results.

And Don Juan, considering this a good example, caused it to be written in this book, and composed the lines, which say thus :—

> Murmur not at God's dealings; it may be
> He seeks thy good, in ways thou canst not see.

NOTES.

Don Manuel, in this tale, while calling upon us to exercise implicit faith and resignation to the will of Providence, as a Christian duty, proves that his mind was not prejudiced by the then prevailing Arab doctrine of fatalism and inert blind submission to what was supposed to be dispensations of Providence, but urges equally the duty of using our intellectual powers that we may be enabled to discriminate between what really is the will of God, and what arises from our own indiscretion, and what does or does not admit of remedy.

CHAPTER XVII.

Concerning that which happened to a great Philosopher and a young King, his Pupil.

COUNT LUCANOR conversed with Patronio, his counsellor, at another time, in the following manner :—

"Patronio," said he, "it happens that I had a relative whom I loved very much, and who was also much attached to me. He left, at his death, a son, still very young, and it devolves upon me to educate this boy, both from the great obligations I am under, as also for the love I had for his father; neither can I forget the great assistance I received from this good friend when I needed it, and which I feel I shall hereafter receive from the son also: and God knows I love him as my own child. Now, as the boy has intelligence, I hope, through God, that he may become a good man; but youths are often led away by bad examples, and fail in doing all that they ought to do. Now, knowing the correctness of your understanding, it would please me much to have your opinion; and I pray you to advise me how I should direct this youth, so that his body, soul, and estate may profit by it."

"Count Lucanor," said Patronio, "in order that you may act as concerns this boy in the manner which appears to me most desirable, I would wish you to hear what happened to a great philosopher, who had a young king for his pupil."

The Count begged he would relate to him what that was.

"My lord," said Patronio, "a king had a son, whom he placed in the charge of a great philosopher to be educated, a man in whom he had great confidence.

"When the king died, his son, the young king, still remained under the care of the philosopher until he was more than fifteen years of age. But soon after this he began to disregard the wise counsels of his preceptor, and to associate with reprobate companions, who, having no interest in his real welfare, flattered and encouraged him in all his wishes.

This conduct caused his manners and habits to become so entirely degenerated that the people began to observe it, and to speak of him, saying, how he was gradually losing the charm and openness of youth.

" The philosopher whose duty it had been to educate the king, seeing this state of things, was much grieved, and thought seriously of it, but felt quite at a loss how to act.   He had tried many times to restrain him by prayers and by gentle means, and often by severe ones, but all without effect.   The philosopher seeing this, and finding that in no way could he induce him to listen to good counsel, thought by means of the following device that he might influence him.   He commenced by gradually circulating about the court that he possessed the art of divining, and to a greater extent than any other man in the world.

"After a time this reached the ears of the king, who asked the philosopher if it were really true that he possessed the art of augury, as they had informed him ?

" This at first he denied ; but, after some further solicitation on the part of the king, he admitted it was so, but expressed great anxiety that it should not be known to the world.

"Youth is usually impatient to know and do all things ; and the king, being young, urgently pressed the philosopher to give him an example of his powers.   The more he excused himself, the more

the young king entreated.   At length the philosopher
proposed that they should one morning leave the
palace together very early, so as not to be observed,
when he would give him an exemplification of his
powers.

"Early the following morning they started, the
philosopher directing his steps towards a valley in
which were a number of deserted villages, where they
heard a crow cawing on a tree.   The king pointed
this out to the philosopher, who made signs for him
to be silent.   Another crow, which they saw on a
neighbouring bough, commenced likewise to caw
from time to time, giving it the appearance of a
conversation.

"After the philosopher had listened some time,
he began to weep bitterly, rent his clothes, and exhibited all the outward signs of violent grief.

"When the youthful king saw this, he was in
great alarm and begged he would tell him what had
occurred to disturb him in that manner.

"The philosopher requested he would not insist
on knowing the cause; but, after much entreaty,
told him, saying, it were better for him that he were
dead than living, feeling so disgraced through his
pupil's conduct; for not only the people, but even
the birds, knew that, from his unjust taxation and
total neglect of his duties, he would lose his kingdom, together with all his possessions, and be
despised by mankind.

"The young king inquired how he could learn

this from the birds; and was told, in reply, that these crows intended marrying the son of the one with the daughter of the other. The crow who commenced speaking first, said to the other, ' It is a long time since this marriage was arranged; it would be better now that it should take place.'

" ' It is true,' said the other crow, 'it was to have been so; but now I have become much richer than you; and, thanks be to God,' said she, ' since the present king began his reign, all the villages in this my valley have become deserted, and I find in the abandoned houses abundance of snakes, lizards, toads, and other things which usually exist in such places; therefore, as I have much more to eat than formerly, the marriage would not now be equal.'

" When the other crow heard this she commenced laughing, and replied, ' What you have said has very little sense in it, if it be all the reason you can give for breaking off the marriage; for, if it pleases God to prolong the life of the young king, my daughter will be very much richer than your son, as there will be many more deserted houses in the valley where we live, we having ten villages where you have only one; you need not, therefore, on this account, delay the marriage.'

" Hearing this explanation, the two crows con- sented at once to the union of their children.

" Now, the young king, hearing all this, was much grieved, and began to reflect how deficient and careless he had been in the proper fulfilment of his duties, by his neglect converting his kingdom into a desert. When his preceptor saw how thoughtful and unhappy he had become, and that he appeared now disposed to listen to advice, he gave him some good instructions; and in this way was his conduct entirely changed, and he devoted himself ever afterwards to improve, not only his own affairs, but those of his kingdom.

"And you, Count Lucanor, since you desire to educate and establish good principles in this youth, let it be done by good examples; by instructive conversations and in agreeable manner lead him to understand and like his duties. But on no account worry him by misjudged chastisements, or think to guide him by ill-treatment, for the disposition of the young is such that they soon acquire a dislike to those who correct them, particularly young men of high, independent spirit, as they will never admit they are in the wrong, although it may be their best friend who corrects them, and with the kindest intentions, yet they never see things in this light. Avoid carefully this method, so injurious to both parties, and so destructive to the happy accomplishment of your wishes."

The Count was much pleased with the advice Patronio gave him, and acted upon it.

And as Don Juan approved of this example, he ordered it to be written in this book, and composed the following verses:—

Do not chastise the erring youth,
But lead him gently to the truth.

NOTES.

This fable is evidently of Eastern origin, and is found in almost all their collections. Although its style seems peculiar to the old Indian, we find in the different relations the birds sometimes represented to be crows; in others, owls; again, as other birds of prey. The first idea has had many imitators, but none have developed it with the good style and clearness of the author of Lucanor. Le Sage relates a very amusing tale, similar to the above, of a conversation between two magpies, without, however, determining its origin. He merely says, "It reminds me of an Indian tale that I read in Pilpay or some other fabulist."

CHAPTER XVIII.

Relates what happened to a Moorish King, who had three Sons, and who desired to know which would become the best Man.

OUNT LUCANOR, being one day in conversation with Patronio, said as follows :—

"Patronio, there are many young men who are being brought up at my court. Some are of high birth, some are not. Now I find their manners and dispositions so various that I am perplexed ; and, knowing the strength of your judgment, I pray you to tell me how I may be able to form an opinion as to which of them will become the best man."

"My lord," said Patronio, "the question which you place before me is very difficult to answer, for we cannot speak with certainty of that which is to come; and, as what you demand is hidden in the future, so must some uncertainty rest upon my opinion.

"But we may be able to form some idea by particularly observing their development internally as well as externally. As regards this latter, there is the form of the features, the grace of movement, the complexion, as also the growth of the body and development of its members; by the principal members, I mean those essential to good health, the heart, the brain, and the liver. Yet though all these signs may appear satisfactory, we can speak with no certainty as to the ultimate results, for seldom do they all accord long, one derangement influencing all the functions, or the contrary. But for the most part, according to the indications above named, may we judge of the future. Notice the form of the features, and particularly the eyes, with the grace of movement: these signs seldom deceive. Do not, however, suppose that gracefulness is dependent upon beauty or ugliness, for there are many men who are handsome and well-formed, but without grace; while again, others, decidedly ill-made, have that gracefulness which entitles them to be

called fine men. Nevertheless, the development of
the body and limbs should be taken as indications of
valour and activity, although it may not be always
so. It is, therefore, as I said before, very difficult to
speak with certainty, for what appears favourable
now may, by the force of circumstances, be entirely
changed. Again, the condition of the mind is still
more difficult to understand, when you seek through
it for indications of what the young man is to become. You require that I should give you some
certain signs whereby you can form an opinion of
which of your young men will become the most
manly. It will much please me to be permitted to
recount to you how, upon a similar occasion, a
Moorish king proved his three sons, to ascertain
which of them would become the bravest man."

"Relate to me," said the Count, "what that
was."

"My lord," said Patronio, "there was a Moorish
king who had three sons. Now he, having the
power to appoint which of them he pleased to reign
after him, when he had arrived at a good old age,
the leading men of his kingdom waited upon him,
praying to be informed which of his sons he would
please to name as his successor. The king replied,
that in one month he would give them an answer.

"After eight or ten days the king said to his
eldest son, 'I shall ride out to-morrow, and I wish
you to accompany me.'

"The son waited upon the king as desired, but

not so early as the time appointed. When he arrived, the king said he wished to dress, and requested him to bring him his garments. His son went to the Lord of the Bedchamber, and requested him to take the king his garments. The attendant inquired what suit it was he wished for; and the son returned to ask his father, who replied, his state robe. The young man went and told the attendant to bring the state robe.

" Now, for every article of the king's attire it was necessary to go backwards and forwards, carrying answers and questions, till at length the attendant came to dress and boot the king. The same repetition goes on when the king called for his horse, spurs, bridle, saddle, sword, and so forth. Now, all being prepared, with some trouble and difficulty, the king changed his mind, and said he would not ride out; but desired the prince his son to go through the city, carefully observing everything worth notice, and that, on his return, he should come and give his father his opinion of what he had seen.

"The prince set out, accompanied by the royal suite and the chief nobility. Trumpets, cymbals, and other instruments preceded this brilliant cavalcade. After traversing a part of the city only, he returned to the palace, when the king desired him to relate what most arrested his attention.

"'I observed nothing, sire,' said he, 'but the great noise caused by the cymbals and trumpets, which confounded me.'

"A few days later, the king sent for his second son, and commanded him to attend very early the next day, when he subjected him to the same ordeal as his brother, but with a somewhat more favourable result.

"Again, after some days, he called for his youngest son's attendance. Now this young man came to the palace very early, long before his father was awake, and waited patiently until the king arose, when he entered his chamber with that respectful humiliation which became him.   The king then desired him to bring his clothes that he might dress. The young prince begged the king to specify which clothes, boots, etc., the same with all the other things he desired, so that he could bring all at the same time, neither would he permit the attendant to assist him, saying, if the king permitted him he would feel highly honoured, and was willing to do all that was required.

"When the king was dressed, he requested his son to bring his horse. Again the son asked what horse, saddle, spurs, sword, and other requisites he desired to have ; and as he commanded so it was done, without trouble or farther annoyance.

"Now, when all was ready, the king, as before, declined going. He, however, requested his son to go, and to take notice of what he saw, so that on his return he might relate to him what he thought worthy of notice.

"In obedience to his father's commands, the

young prince rode through the city, attended by the same escort as his brothers; but they knew nothing, neither did the younger son, nor indeed anyone else, of the object the king had in view. As he rode along, he desired that they would show him the interior of the city, the streets, and where the king kept his treasures, and what was supposed to be the amount thereof; he inquired where the nobility and people of importance in the city lived; after this, he desired that they should present to him all the cavalry and infantry, and these he made go through their evolutions; he afterwards visited the walls, towers, and fortresses of the city, so that when he returned to the king it was very late.

"The king desired him to tell him what he had seen. The young prince replied, that he feared giving offence if he stated all he felt at what he had seen and observed. Now the king commanded him to relate everything, as he hoped for his blessing. The young man replied, that although he was sure his father was a very good king, yet it seemed to him he had not done as much good as he might, having such good troops, so much power, and such great resources; for, had he wished it, he might have made himself master of the world.

"Now the king felt much pleased at this judicious remark of his son. So when the time arrived that he had to give his decision to the people, he told them that he should appoint his youngest son for their king, from the indications he had given him of his ability, by certain proofs of fitness to govern, to which he had subjected all his sons, although he would have desired to appoint his eldest son as his successor ; yet he felt it a duty to select the one who appeared best qualified for the station.

"And you, Count Lucanor, if you desire to know which of the young men is the most promising, you must reflect on what I have related to you, and, by the adoption of similar means, you will be enabled to form your opinion."

The Count was much pleased with what Patronio had said ; and, as Don Juan found this to be a good example, he ordered it to be written in this book, and made the following lines, which say :—

> By ways and works thou mayest know
> Which youths to worthiest men will grow.

NOTES.

This interesting narrative, evidently of Arabic origin, recalls to us the heroic tale related in the history of Rodrigo Diaz de Vivar, commonly called the Cid Campeador. This interesting tale is immortalized by Corneille in one of his best plays. The story is as follows. The old Count Diego de Vivar, after the gross insult he received from Count D'Orgaz, called his three sons to him, and forcibly pressed their hands within his own. Now the two elder ones, Fernando and Bermuda, shrieked out as if they had been seized by the gripe of a lion, whilst Rodrigo, the younger, gave no indication of pain, but uttered an exclamation, and said, 'If you were not my father I would strike you." To which the old Count replied, "It would not be the first blow I have received. You now know the offence ; see here is the sword ; I have nothing further to add. With

my white hairs I go to weep over my insulted honour, leaving
you, my son, the duty to avenge it." The sentence uttered by
the old Count, addressing his son, as written by Corneille, is
truly beautiful, when with impassioned dignity he exclaims,
"Rodrique, as-tu du cœur?" ("Rodrigo, have you a heart?")

With more discernment, Don Manuel, who has probably
taken this historical fact as the foundation of his own story,
with this difference, however, that in his recital he relies, not
as the Cid, upon physical indications, but after due investiga-
tions, as is shown in his narrative, places his reliance more
upon the reasoning powers and mental development of, as in
the case of Diego, the younger son.

CHAPTER XIX.

*Of that which happened to the Canons of the Cathe-
dral Church of Paris, and to the Friars of Saint
Francis, called Minors.*

COUNT LUCANOR, conversing one day
with Patronio his counsellor, said as
follows :—

"Patronio, I have a friend, with
whom I have arranged to do a certain thing, which
we anticipate will be to our mutual advantage and
honour.   An opportunity now presents itself to commence this undertaking; but, my friend being at
present absent, I feel uncertain how to act until he
returns.   Now, as it has pleased God to bless you
with a good understanding, I pray you to give me
your advice."

"My lord," said Patronio, "if you would act as it appears to me the most advisable for your interest, I should like you to know what happened to the canons of the cathedral church of Paris, with a convent of friars minors."

The Count begged him to relate what it was.

"The canons of the cathedral said, that, as they were the superior order in the church, they had the right to toll the first morning bell. The friars contended that, as they were obliged to rise very early to study, and then to sing matins, they ought more properly to toll the first bell, and wait for no one. All this caused much contention and disputing, both parties expending large sums of money on lawyers and legal documents, the litigation continuing a very long time at the papal court.

"At length a mandate arrived, referring the matter to a cardinal, with an express command that he should promptly decide the question at issue.

"The cardinal ordered all the documents of the case to be placed before him : the multiplicity of these was enough to frighten any man. Now, after having arranged the papers in order, he cited the interested parties to appear before him on a given day to receive sentence. When they assembled before him, he, in their presence, burnt all the writings, and said, 'Friends, the cause has gone on long enough, costing you both much trouble and money; I will therefore discontinue the suit, giving as a final

8

sentence, that they who rise first shall toll the morning bell.'

"And you, Count Lucanor, if the project is
advantageous to both, and you are able to do it
alone, I should advise you not to lose your op
portunity, but act with promptness and decision.
Things are often irretrievably lost by hesitation and
uncalled-for delay, so that afterwards, when a man
desires to act, he finds himself incapable of so doing."

The Count, considering this to be very good advice,
acted upon it, and found the results to answer well.
And Don Juan, understanding that this was a good
example, had it inscribed in this book, and composed
the following verse :—

> The good occasion—use it,
> Lest, through delay, you lose it !

NOTES.

The above tale resembles not a little the facetious style generally adopted by the Archpriest of Hita, Juan Ruiz, famous
for his satirical writings, and a contemporary of Don Juan
Manuel, and by Rabelais. These two writers were particularly
noted for their satirical allegories. The cardinal, in his refined
satire, not only lanced a tacit condemnation against the indo-
lence of the canons, but against also the arbitrary and unjust
claim set up by them, in contesting with an inferior class that
right to which industry and early rising clearly entitled them.

CHAPTER XX.

*Of that which happened to a Falcon and a Heron,
and, more particularly, to a cunning Falcon, which
belonged to the Infant Don Manuel.*

OUNT LUCANOR conversed one day
with his counsellor, Patronio, in the
manner following :—

"Patronio," said he, "it has hap-
pened lately to me to have contentions with many
men, and no sooner is one quarrel ended than I am
by some one instigated to commence another ; others
again recommend me to rest and be at peace, while
again, others wish me to renew the war with the
Moors. Now, knowing that no one is better able
than yourself to advise me, I pray that you will
counsel me how best to act under these circumstances."

"My lord," said Patronio, "in order that you
may the better act with judgment, it would be well
that you should know what happened to a cunning
falcon, belonging to the Infant Don Manuel."

The Count begged that he would relate the circumstance.

"Count Lucanor," said Patronio, "the Infant
Don Manuel being one day at the chase in the
country near Escalona let fly a cunning falcon at a

heron. Scarcely had he mounted above the heron,
than he perceived an eagle approaching, when the
falcon, being in great fear of him, left the heron and
took to flight. The eagle, finding that he could not
overtake the falcon, gave up the chase. As soon as
the falcon saw that the eagle had departed he
renewed his pursuit of the heron ; which the eagle
perceiving, turned again upon the falcon, when the
falcon again took flight as before, pursued by the
eagle, which soon gave up the chase, when immediately
the falcon returned to chase the heron. This occurred
three or four times, the eagle departing each time, as
before, and each time returning to kill the falcon.

"The falcon, perceiving that the eagle rendered
his killing the heron impossible, he mounted above
the eagle and descended upon him with great fierce-
ness, wounding him several times, until he drove
him away. No sooner was he gone than he flew
in pursuit of the heron and was engaged with it
very high in air, which the eagle perceiving, again
returned to attack him. The falcon, seeing that all
his attempts were frustrated, left the heron, and
mounted again above the eagle, descending upon him
with such violence that he broke his wing. Seeing
the eagle fall to the ground with the wing broken,
the falcon then went in pursuit of the heron, and
killed it this time, having freed himself from the
hindrance of the eagle.

"And you, Count Lucanor, since you desire to
know how best to act as regards your estate, your

honour, and your soul, and how best to devote yourself to the service of God, can anything in the world
be more proper, considering your position, than
going to war with the Moors, for the glory of the
holy and true catholic faith? Therefore, as soon as
you can liberate yourself from other parties, commence a war with the Moors, as much good must
arise from it. Firstly, you are devoting yourself to
the service of God in an honourable engagement,
gaining renown, and not eating the bread of idleness,
which should never be said of a powerful noble.
And, moreover, those holding your position, and
without occupation, are unable to appreciate the
worth of those who surround them, who lose the
reward which, if engaged, they might otherwise
deserve. Idleness may also incline you to do that
which might be better left alone. Since, therefore,
it is good and profitable that you, holding the position you do, should be well employed, certain it is
that nothing can be better, more honourable, and
more to your advantage here and hereafter than a
war with the Moors.

"Reflect, at least, on the example I gave you of
the leap made by Richard, King of England, and
how much he gained by it. And remember in your
heart that you must die, and that God is all-seeing
and of great justice, and that you cannot escape the
great punishment due to you for those sins which
you have committed unless indeed you should be fortunate enough to have an opportunity to do penance

for your sins. So if, being at war with the Moors, you were slain, being at the time truly penitent, you would have the good fortune of being a martyr ; and if you were not killed in battle, your good works and your good intentions would save you."

The Count considered this a good example, and determined in his heart to follow it. He prayed to God to direct him how best to carry out his wishes.

And Don Juan, understanding that this example was very good, ordered it to be written in this book, and made these lines, which say as follows :—

> God's guidance making thee secure,
> Fight on to the end, of victory sure.

NOTE.

This original and amusing tale of Don Manuel appears to be written by the hand of an old hunter, and has not only a war-like but a political signification, illustrating the necessity of exercising our ingenuity, judgment, and steady resolution to overcome opposition, losing not the opportunity, if presented, to soar above, and, like the falcon, overwhelm by the force of well-directed determination what before appeared invincible.

CHAPTER XXI.

Recounts what happened to Count Ferran Gonzalez, and the Reply which he gave to his Vassals.

COUNT LUCANOR returned one day from a campaign, much wearied and quite overcome with fatigue, his treasury being also literally empty; and in this state, before he could enjoy any repose, he received intelligence that another attack was about to be made upon him. Now, the greater number of his vassals, hearing this, strongly advised him to rest and recruit his exhausted strength, and then act as circumstances might dictate.

Now the Count begged of Patronio to advise him, and this latter replied that, in his opinion, the best way to do this would be by relating to him the answer Count Ferran Gonzalez once gave to his vassals.

" The Count Ferran Gonzalez conquered Almarzon in Hacinas, and lost there very many of his troops, he himself and the survivors being badly wounded. Now, before they had recovered from their fatigues and wounds, the Count was informed that the King of Navarre had entered his dominions, and he immediately summoned his vassals to prepare themselves to attack those of Navarre. To this they replied, that both themselves and their horses were too fatigued, and, although desirous to do their duty as usual, yet being wounded as well as the Count himself, they hoped they should be allowed to rest until they were recovered.

"When the Count saw they were all of the same mind, being himself more influenced by his honour than his sufferings, replied, 'Friends, for the wounds which we have, let us not desert our duty; remember, those we may receive will serve but to make us forget the old ones.'

"His people, seeing that he was devoid of all personal considerations, and influenced only by a sense of honour and love of his country, went with him and gained the battle, after which they had a long continuance of peace.

"And you, Count Lucanor, if you are really desirous of doing that which you ought to do, seeing how much is required for the defence of your country, of your people, and of your honour, do not remain inactive because of your unhappy position, or your fatigue, or from a sense of danger, for the new enterprise will serve but to make you forget the troubles which are passed."

And the Count, considering this to be a good example and very good advice, followed it, and found the result favourable.

And Don Juan, understanding that this tale was worthy a place in this book, had it written therein, and composed the following verses :—

Hold this for sure, for 'tis a truth well proved,
Honour and slothful ease are wide removed.

NOTES.

Don Manuel has in this tale exemplified the turbulence of the feudal system of the middle ages. The fable belongs to the tenth century, when every sovereign of lesser rank was little better than a party chief; and had full scope for the exercise of his virtues as well as his vices. The moral tone of society was reduced to so low an ebb that by force of opposition individual characters appear ennobled. The proximity of a race so inimical in their characters and religion to their Spanish neighbours ever increased the peril of these civil commotions. It was necessary to go continually from frontier to frontier to arrange, by the sword or otherwise, petty disputes. So each lord and chief was forced to a constant display of courage and activity. Where can we find anything nobler than the reply of Ferran Gonzalez, as given in this story, unless that of the French hero, Christian and philosopher of the 16th century, when he said, " *La vie est une lutte, ne perdons pas un seul jour ; nous nous reposerons dans l'éternité* " ?

The above story has been translated, as a specimen, by Ticknor, in his " History of Spanish Literature," vol. i., pp. 62-68, and is, with one exception to be mentioned hereafter, the only portion of the work which had ever up to this time (as far as I am aware) appeared in English.

CHAPTER XXII.

Of that which happened to a King and his Favourite.

HEN Count Lucanor was once in confidential conversation with Patronio, his adviser, he said, "Patronio, a man of rank, much honoured and of great influence, and who, you must know, is a particular friend of mine, a few days since informed me, in strict confidence, that, from circumstances which have occurred, he had determined upon leaving this country never to return ; and, in testimony of the great regard which he has for me, he desires to leave me all his lands—those which he has purchased, as also those which he holds on tenure. It appears to be a great honour as well as very advantageous to me ; yet I pray you to tell me what you think of it, and how I ought to act under such circumstances."

"Count Lucanor," said Patronio, "your own good sense needs but little of my advice ; but, since you desire my opinion of the matter, let me caution you against being deceived. In the first place, I would say, that however much you may consider this man as your friend, I am of opinion his object is to deceive you ; indeed, your position

calls to my mind that which, under similar circumstances, happened to a king and his favourite."

Count Lucanor desired to be informed what that
was ; and Patronio related it as follows :—

" There was a king, who had a favourite in whom
he had great confidence, which excited the jealousy
of those around, so that they sought every opportunity to speak evil of him to the king, his lord.
Nevertheless, with all their statements, the king
could not be induced to suspect or doubt his loyalty.
Seeing that they were in no way able to accomplish
what they desired, they informed the king that his
favourite was plotting to bring about his death, and
as to a young son that the king had, as soon as he
had him in his power, he intended to destroy him,
and so possess himself of the kingdom.

" It was not until the king heard this that he en-
tertained any doubt as to the loyalty of his favourite,
but now he was sorely grieved, and was not without
fear ; for in such cases, where there is so much to
lose and so much to be gained, no prudent man can
hope to act rightly without proof; and therefore
the king remained overwhelmed with doubt and
suspicion and in great fear, not knowing how to
act until he really knew the truth, for he knew there
were those who sought evil against his favourite.

"The courtiers, seeing the king's anxiety, came
to him and informed him of an ingenious method,
by which he would be enabled to prove the truth of
what they had asserted.

"After hearing them, the king thought well of their suggestions, and acted upon them. Some few days after, the king, conversing with his favourite, gave him to understand by degrees that he was much disgusted with the life of this world, in which all appeared as vanity; saying no more to him on this occasion. At the end of some days, while talking again with him, he remarked, as if by accident, that each day made him more dislike the life and manners of the world, and so often repeated the same thing until at last the favourite was impressed with the conviction that the king really had no enjoyment in the honours, or riches, or pleasures of this world. And when the king saw that he was fully impressed with this feeling, he said to him, one day, 'I have been reflecting upon the subject which occupies my thoughts, and have come to the determination to resign my kingdom, and retire into a distant country, where I am not known and where I can enjoy the pleasure of retirement and peace, and where I can do penance for my sins, and so obtain the mercy and grace of God, fitting me for the glory of Paradise.'

"When the favourite heard these words of the king, he was much astonished, and used every argument to divert him from his intentions; and, among others, how unjustly he would be acting towards God, in leaving his people, amongst whom now there was peace and justice; for it was quite certain that as soon as he had departed the country would be torn by revolutions and contentions, doing great injury to the cause of God, and to the kingdom, and, above all, said he, 'you cannot with justice leave the queen and your son, who is still so young, exposed (as they certainly will be) to so much danger, both as regards their persons and their estates.'

"To this the king replied, 'I have well considered in my mind how best I shall be able to leave my kingdom well protected, as also my wife and son, and maintain order in the land. You know that I have raised you to your present position, and have rendered you great service. In return, I have ever found you loyal; you have always served me well and with rectitude. For these reasons, I feel assured I can leave the queen and my son with you in greater safety than with any other man in the world. I therefore consign them to your care, with all the fortresses and provinces of my kingdom, convinced that no harm can come to them, or treachery to my son; and if I should ever return, I feel certain of finding safe all I have left in your charge; and if, perchance, I should die, I have equal confidence that you will guard and protect my son until the time comes when he is able to govern the kingdom. It is for these reasons that I feel I can leave well protected all that I possess.'

"When the counsellor found that it was impossible to divert the king from his intentions, and heard that the queen and her son were to be left in his charge, he could not conceal the gratification he felt in having full power to act as he pleased.

" Now he had in his house a captive, who was a very wise man and a philosopher, and whom he was accustomed to consult in all important matters. As soon, therefore, as he parted from the king, he sought his captive and recounted to him what the king had said, and how gratified he felt in the good fortune of having the queen, and her son, and all the kingdom placed under his entire control.

" When the captive philosopher heard all that had passed between his lord and the king, he blamed him very much for accepting the king's proposals, saying that he felt certain he had placed himself and his possessions in great danger, ' for, whatever the king may have said, it is not his intention to do so; his only object is to verify the suspicions which your enemies have impressed on his mind ; and by letting him see that you are pleased by his proposal, you have placed yourself in great danger.'

" When the counsellor of the king heard this explanation he was in great trouble, for he now saw clearly that everything was as his captive had said. And when the wise man whom he kept in his house saw him in such great distress, he counselled him in what manner he might escape from the danger in which he was placed, and this was the way. He was that night to shave off his hair and beard and clothe himself in an old and patched garment, such as is worn by wandering beggars, and with a staff and a pair of old broken shoes well ironed and gaping open, and to put between the lining of his

clothes a quantity of gold pieces. In this way, at
the break of day, he appeared at the gate of the king,
and desired the porter who was there to inform the
king secretly that he was prepared to depart with
him, before the people were awake. The porter
was astonished to see him come in that style to have
an interview with the king, but did as he desired.

"The king marvelled much at this message, and
desired his favourite to enter. When he saw him
he was astonished, and requested to be informed
why he presented himself in that style of dress.

"The counsellor replied that, knowing his determination to travel into a foreign country, and that
he so desired it that no persuasion could alter his
resolution ; and, as all the honour and wealth which
he possessed were derived from the king, and seeing
the misery and expatriation he had determined to
undergo, even to the leaving of his queen, his son,
and his kingdom, he had resolved to travel with him,
and to serve him with an unceasing fidelity. He
had assumed the dress in which he presented himself
in order that they might travel unknown, and having
placed gold enough in his vest to serve both their
lives, he ventured to suggest that they should immediately depart, before their intentions could be
known.

"When the king heard what his favourite had
said, believing in his true loyalty, he expressed himself much pleased, and related the manner in which
he had been deceived, and that what he had said

was but to prove his sincerity.   And the counsellor
thanked God that he had taken the advice of the
philosopher whom he held as a captive in his house.

"And you, Count Lucanor, must take care not
to be deceived by this offer of your friend, for certain
it is that he only makes it to test your feelings, as
to your desiring to possess yourself of his honour
and possessions.   Assure him, to the contrary, that
you desire neither the one nor the other; for without confidence, friendship cannot continue long."

And the Count thought well of the advice which
Patronio gave, and, following it, found the end
beneficial.

And Don Juan, considering this example to be
very good, caused it to be written in this book, and
composed these lines :—

> Do not believe that a man will descend
> To dishonour himself for the good of a friend.

And these others which say :—

> By the pity of God, and a good counsel in need,
> A man shall from danger escape, and succeed.

NOTE.

In this example, the moralist and courtier, Don Manuel,
gives us two distinct lessons, the principal of which is addressed
to court favourites, and, we suspect, the fruit of his own experience, he having passed the greater part of his life in constant
trouble and anxiety, caused by the perfidy of Alfonso XI, who
was continually laying snares for him, though, being more enlightened than his master, he knew how to evade them.   In

many Indian and Arabian tales we find examples of the constant struggle going on between kings and favourites. In those
states where despotism reigned, ambition was always urging
men to dangerous stratagems; the art exemplified in such cannot astonish us more than the multiplicity of plots arising from
the natural distrust of the Asiatic character.

CHAPTER XXIII.

*What happened to a good Man and his Son,
leading a beast to market.*

N another occasion, when Count Lucanor was conversing with Patronio, his
adviser, he informed him that he felt
much embarrassed as to the method of
carrying out an object which he had in view, for
he felt that in whatever way he acted many people
would criticise and blame him, some with reason
and some without.

"How shall I act?" said the Count. "I pray
you to inform me what you would advise under the
circumstances."

"Count Lucanor," said Patronio, "I know that
you can find many men more able to advise you than
I am; besides, God has blessed you with a good
understanding, making my advice but of little service
to you; but, since it is your desire that I should give
you my opinion how to act, I shall have much
pleasure in being permitted to recount what once

happened, under similar circumstances, to a man and his son."

The Count expressing his desire to be informed what that was, Patronio related as follows :—

" A good man had a son, who, although young, had so excellent an understanding that the father was induced to consult him in all his projects. The son, however, had no decision or perseverance in his character; and whatever the father proposed, so many doubts and objections were raised by the son that each project was abandoned and it ended by nothing being done.

" It is well known that, although the young may not be deficient in understanding and spirit, yet they may commit many errors : having a mind to see the right thing to be done, but, wanting perseverance and a good guide, never complete anything. And so this young man, though he had a naturally good understanding, yet, wanting the resolution to complete anything, caused his father much trouble in many of his undertakings.

" For a long time the father submitted to this state of things, suffering much injury from being interfered with in his projects, and annoyance from many things which his son said to him. At length he determined to punish his son, and give him an example by showing him how he managed his own affairs when not interfered with, as we are told by eye-witnesses.

" The good man and his son were farmers, living

in the neighbourhood of a town. One market-day he told him they should both go there to buy some things which were wanted. They agreed to take a beast to bring back the goods; and accordingly went to market, leading the beast. On their way they met some men returning from the town. After saluting, these latter remarked how strange it was that they should lead the beast and walk. The good man asked his son what he thought of the remarks made by the men. The son replied that what they said was just, for the animal being unladen it was silly for them to be walking. The good man then told his son to mount, and so journeying they met other men, who commenced saying, 'How is it that the old man, who appears fatigued, should be walking while the young man is riding?' Again the good man asked his son what he thought of this remark; again he replied that he thought they were right. The father then told his son to dismount, and mounted in his stead. A little way further they met some people who observed how unjust it appeared that the old man, who was accustomed to hardships, should be riding like a gentleman, while he allowed his son, who was young and delicate, to walk. Again the good man inquired of his son what he now thought; he replied that he agreed with them. On this the good man desired his son to mount also, so that neither should walk. Again they met others, who remarked to them that they were committing a great error in both riding on a beast so thin and appa-

rently so ill able to bear them. Again the good
man demanded of his son what he thought of these
last remarks. The youth replied, it certainly appeared to him that what they said was true.

" Then the father answered his son, saying, 'Son,
remember when we left home we led the beast unladen, which you thought was best. After meeting
some men on the road, who made remarks on our
walking, I ordered you to mount, you then agreed
with them. We met, afterwards, other men, who
said that was not right, in which you also agreed. I
then ordered you to dismount, and mounted in your
stead; and, forsooth, because others remarked on
my riding and your walking, I ordered you to mount
with me; and this also you thought was the best.
And now, because others said we were both wrong
in riding, you concur with them. Such being the
case, I beg of you to tell me what it is possible to
do that will not admit of being criticised. We were
both walking, and they said we were wrong; I
walked and you rode, again we erred; then I rode
on the beast and you walked, this was judged wrong.
Hence, you see, it is not possible, do what you will,
to avoid criticism. And this I give you as an
example, so certain am I that no action, however
worthy, will be thought well of by all. If the
action is good, the ill-disposed will find some fault
with it; and if it is an evil action, the good must
certainly condemn it. So while you endeavour
conscientiously to do your best, still many will speak

of you and judge your actions according to their own views.'

"And now, Count Lucanor, what is it you desire to do and yet fear what the people may say, whether you do it or do it not? Since you command me to advise you, my counsel is this, before commencing the undertaking, look at the good and evil which may follow, taking care that your own inclinations do not mislead you; and seek the advice of those who are of sound understanding and well informed. If such an adviser is not to be met with, take care that you proceed carefully and justly, allowing a day and a night to pass before carrying out your determination, that is, if time permits, carefully avoiding being influenced by the feeling of what people might say of you."

The Count found Patronio's advice good; and, acting accordingly, all ended well.

And Don Juan, approving of this example, ordered it to be written in this book, and composed the following lines, which are an abbreviation of the whole moral; and the lines are :—

In thy chosen life's adventure, stedfastly pursue the cause,
Neither moved by critic's censure, nor the multitude's applause.

NOTES.

This is a well-known fable in all languages. Although Don Manuel's may not be the first, there is yet much that is original in its detail. La Fontaine's fable of "The Miller, his Son, and the Ass," book the third, fable the first, is preceded by a prologue, wherein he tells us that he has taken his subject from the life of Malherbe, a writer of the sixteenth century, wherein Malherbe represents himself, like Patronio, giving advice to Racan, his friend but superior in station, who, like Count Lucanor, informs him how undecided he is as to his future course of life. The answer given is the fable above named, which bears an exact resemblance to Don Manuel's, except in the conclusion. The narrative given in this fable first reappears in the Turkish romance, entitled, "The Forty Viziers," where it figures under the title of "The Gardener, his Son, and an Ass." This work belongs to the fifteenth century, and its author acknowledges to have taken his idea from an ancient Arabian tale, by *Cheikh Zadé*, entitled, "*Hikaiat Arbaïn Sebah wamesa*,"—" Forty Mornings and Forty Evenings," which latter is derived from the "Book of Sindabah," an Indian romance. This last was translated from Sanscrit into Persian, from that into Arabic, then into Syriac, then into Hebrew. This has served for the Latin work composed towards the end of the twelfth or the beginning of the thirteenth century, under the title of "*Historia Septem Sapientium Romœ*," by Jehans, a monk of Hauteselve, from whence four modern translations are extant, amongst them the French one of 1492, whence Malherbe doubtless derived the subject.

CHAPTER XXIV.

Of what a Genovese said to his soul when about to die.

OUNT LUCANOR, conversing one day with Patronio, said, "Thank God! I feel happy with myself and at peace with all the world. Now I am advised to undertake a dangerous pilgrimage, and I am disposed to follow this advice. Such is my confidence, however, in you, that before commencing the undertaking I desire to have your opinion as to its advisability."

"My lord," said Patronio, "in order to know what is most incumbent on you, I should like you to hear what happened to a Genovese when communing with his soul."

The Count desired him to relate what that was.

Patronio replied, "My lord, there was a Genovese who was very rich, and highly esteemed by his neighbours, who, finding himself at the point of death, assembled all his friends and relations, and, as soon as they arrived, sent for his wife and children, and had himself conveyed to a splendid palace, from whence there was a prospect of earth and sea, and ordered all his treasures and jewels to be brought

before him; and when all were before him, he began
to speak in a cheerful manner saying, 'My soul, so
you wish to leave me. I cannot tell why; if it is
that you desire wife and children, here they are,
and such as you ought to be proud of; if it is that
you long for friends and relations, here they are,
both good and honourable; if it is gold and silver,
precious stones, jewels, and merchandise that you
desire, you have them here in abundance; if you
desire vessels and galleys to bring you honour and
treasures from afar, behold them on the sea; if you
desire lands or beautiful gardens, look on them from
these windows; if it is horses, and mules, and dogs,
for hunting or amusement, you wish, or players to
entertain you; or if it is luxurious rooms, beds, and
furniture, or any of the many things that are desirable in this life, of all these you have a super-
abundance. Since you have all that makes life
desirable, and are not contented therewith, but seek
for what you know not, go therefore to God.'

"And you, my lord, since, thanks be to God!
you are at peace—happy and honoured, take care
how you risk your present happiness, in following
the advice of those who desire only to engage you
in an undertaking which makes you amenable to
their wills. They are now submissive to you while
you are at home and at peace; but being away, they
may avail themselves of the opportunity to increase
their possessions, which they cannot do so long as
you live peaceably and quietly, corroborating that

which the Genovese said to his soul. My advice, therefore, to you is, so long as you can enjoy peace, comfort, and honour, not to risk them by unrequired adventures."

The Count was well pleased with Patronio's advice, followed it, and prospered.

And Don Juan, although liking this moral, did not make a verse as usual, but contented himself by applying to it the old Castilian proverb of—

"Who is well sitting, let him not rise."

NOTE.

I believe this to be an original fable, as no source has yet been found from which it is supposed to be derived.

The yearning of the soul after something more enduring than worldly treasures has been finely expressed by Don Juan, in this chapter. Probably it has even deeper meanings than he himself knew.

CHAPTER XXV.

What happened to the Crow, with the Fox.

ANOTHER time, Count Lucanor, speaking with Patronio, said, "A man who pretends to be my friend began praising me very much, and for the regard he has for me desires to conduct a law-suit for the obtaining of property which at first sight appears to be my right." And the Count related the circumstances of the law-suit to Patronio, and how advantageous it appeared to him.

Patronio, seeing the deceit which lay hidden under plausible words, said, "Count Lucanor, know that this man is deceiving you, wishing to make you believe that your power and position is greater than it really is ; and in order to avoid falling into this snare allow me to tell you what happened to a crow with a fox."

The Count asked what that was.

" My lord," replied Patronio, " a crow, happening to find a large piece of cheese, flew up into a tree, in order to eat it without fear or interruption from any one. As soon as he had settled there a fox passed by at the foot of the tree, and, seeing the cheese which the crow held, began to think how he could get possession of it.

" He addressed the crow thus, ' My lord crow, for a long time I have heard marvellous tales of your nobility and your appearance, and, although I have sought you long, it was not the will of Providence that I should meet you until to-day, and seeing you now, find your merits have been much underrated ; and, to convince you I am no flatterer, I will tell you my real opinion of your merits, likewise what others say of you. People say that the colour of your wings, eyes, bill, and claws is approaching to black. Now, as a blackish thing is not so becoming as any other, people make little of your appearance, not seeing how they err in doing so. It is true your wings are black, but so brilliant that they would shame an Indian peacock, the handsomest bird in the world. What matter if your eyes are black, since black eyes are considered so handsome; and what use is an eye unless to see with; and as everything black is most attractive, black eyes are the best—those of the gazelle being the most admired, and the darkest possessed by any animal. Again, your bill, feet, and claws are stronger than those of any other bird of your size. Your flight also is light, as you can go against the strongest wind more easily than any other bird.* I hold that God, who does all things well, would never allow you to be wanting in any accomplishment, so I cannot believe but that you sing as well as any other bird. Now, since God has permitted me to see you, and I find you so superior to anything that has been said of you, only allow me to hear you sing and I shall consider myself happy.'

"Now, my lord, you will observe that the intention of the fox was to deceive the crow by flattering

---

* The exact contrary, of course, being the case, as a poet who has left few appearances of nature unnoticed, has forcibly said :—

> "To-night the winds begin to rise,
> And roar from yonder dropping day :
> The last red leaf is whirl'd away,
> The rooks are blown about the skies."
>
> In Memoriam, xv. I.

him with the appearance of truth ; and be assured that the most dangerous and mortal injuries are those where deceit most resembles truth. When the crow heard how skilfully the fox praised him, he believed as truth everything he said, and thought him his friend, not suspecting it was all done with the object of possessing himself of the cheese he held in his bill. Having heard so much, he at last yielded to the entreaties of the fox, and, opening his bill for the purpose of singing, dropped the cheese, which the fox immediately seized and departed. Thus the crow was deceived by the fox, believing, by his flattery, that he possessed more beauty and accomplishments than he really had.

"And you, Count Lucanor, knowing that Providence has been bountiful to you, should see by this that the man is endeavouring to make you believe that you have more power and are more honoured than you know to be the fact. Be on your guard, therefore, against his deceit."

The Count was pleased by what Patronio said, took his advice, and so avoided a serious error.

Don Juan, judging this a very good example, ordered it to be written in this book, and composed the following verses, which sum up in a few words the entire moral of the story, and say as follows :—

> Who praises you for what you have not
> Seeks to deprive you of what you have got.

NOTE TO CHAPTER XXV.

The outline of this fable will be found in Babrius, i. 77.

ΚΟΡΑΞ ΚΑΙ ΑΛΩΠΗΞ

Κόραξ δεδηχὼς στόματι τυρὸν εἰστήκει·
τυροῦ δ' ἀλώπηξ ἰχανῶσα κερδῴη
μύθῳ τὸν ὄρνιν ἠπάτησε τοιούτῳ·
" κόραξ, καλαί σοι πτέρυγες, ὀξέη γλήνη,
" θηητὸς αὐχήν· στέρνον ἀετοῦ φαίνεις·
" ὄνυξι πάντων θηρίων κατισχύεις·
" ὁ τοῖος ὄρνις κωφὸς ἐσσὶ κοὐ κρώζεις ! "
κόραξ δ' ἐπαίνῳ καρδίην ἐχαυνώθη,
στόματος δὲ τυρὸν ἐκβαλὼν ἐκεκράγει.
τὸν ἢ σοφὴ λαβοῦσα κερτόμῳ γλώσσῃ,
" οὐκ ἦσθ' ἄφωνος," εἶπεν, " ἀλλὰ φωνήεις.
" ἔχεις, κόραξ, ἄπαντα· νοῦς δέ σοι λείπει."

Thus translated by the Rev. James Davies, (p. 68).

THE FOX AND THE CROW.

A crow upon his perch was munching cheese,
When a sly fox, by arguments like these,
To suit herself, beguiled him of his prize :—
" Fair are thy plumes, good crow, and bright thine eyes,
" Charming thy neck, an eagle's breast thou hast,
" In talons thou art by no brute surpass'd.
" 'Tis strange that dumb should be a bird so smart ! "
The flattered crow became elate in heart,
And, cawing, from his mouth the cheese let fall ;
This Reynard snatch'd, and tauntingly did call,
" 'Tis true thou wast not dumb, for thou canst speak,
" Yet, spite of all thou hast, thy mind is weak."

CHAPTER XXVI.

What happened to the Swallow, with the other birds,
when he saw the flax sown.

OUNT LUCANOR, conversing one day with Patronio, spoke thus:—

"Patronio, they tell me that my more powerful neighbours are plotting together and using all their influence to deceive and injure me. I do not, however, myself believe it. Still, knowing your prudence, I wish to ask you what you think I ought to do in this matter."

"My lord," said Patronio, "in order that you may better understand your duty in this case, permit me to relate to you what happened to the swallow and the other birds."

The Count requested to be informed what that was; and Patronio spoke thus:—

"My lord, a swallow one day saw a man sowing flax, and perceived that if the flax grew up men would be enabled with the thread produced therefrom to make nets wherewith to catch birds; so when the sowing was completed, this swallow assembled all the other birds and informed them how the man had sown the flax, also telling them that when the seed came to perfection it would probably be used to injure them.

"Now his advice was, that before the seed commenced growing, and while it was not attached to the earth, they should root it up and destroy it, as it would be very difficult to do so afterwards.

"The birds thought but little of this advice, although he urged it many times, and were not disposed to act. Now the flax so grew that the birds could not uproot it either with their claws or their bills. When the birds found this to be the case, they regretted not having taken the advice of the swallow to avert the injury now inevitable; but, alas! it was too late.

"Now when the swallow saw the birds would not assist him to avert the common danger, he went to the man, and, placing himself under his protection, obtained from him, for himself and his progeny, a promise of future security; and since that time we see that the swallows are safe with men, whilst the other birds are daily caught in nets.

"And you, my lord, if you wish to avert the danger which you think threatens you, remember the saying of the wise man, "when you perceive a threatened danger use every precaution to avert it, for he is not a sensible man who only sees the danger after it has come upon him; but wise is he who by a slight sign or movement forsees the approaching evil, and provides against it.'"

The Count was much pleased with this narrative of Patronio's, and, acting according to his advice, found it prosper.

And as Don Juan approved of this example, he ordered it to be written in this book, and composed the following lines, which say :—

> Wouldst thou make sure from danger to escape,
> Then wait not till it take a threatening shape.

NOTE.

This tale is found in Æsop, and La Fontaine has made it the subject of one of his prettiest fables. But there is a point in the prose apologue of Don Manuel, and in an apologue in verse by his contemporary, Juan Ruiz de Hita, which La Fontaine has missed. This lies in the decision of the swallow to seek the protection of men and frequent their dwellings.

CHAPTER XXVII.

Relates what happened to a Man who carried a very precious Treasure hung round his neck, and who had to pass a River.

NE day Count Lucanor said to Patronio, " It is requisite that I should visit a distant part of the country, where I have to receive a large sum of money, which I can employ advantageously here,

and having great fear that in returning I may be
exposed to much personal danger, I ask for your
advice how to act."

"My lord," said Patronio, "in order that you
may better understand how to act in this emergency,
allow me to tell you what happened to a man who
had to convey a treasure across a river, and which
he carried round his neck."

The Count desired him to proceed, which Patronio did in the following manner :—

"My lord, this man had to pass a very wide and
muddy river ; and there was no alternative, there
being neither bridge, nor boat, nor any other means of
transit, but that of passing through the water. So,
taking off his shoes, he found that with their weight
and that of the treasure which he carried it was
difficult to avoid sinking, the mud increasing as he
reached the centre of the river.

"The king, and an attendant who stood on the
opposite bank, called out to him in a loud voice
to throw away the load which he carried, otherwise
he would be lost.

"The foolish man, little thinking that if he sank
he would lose not only his treasure but his own life
also, would not follow the advice given him by the
king who stood on the opposite shore. As the
current was very strong and the mud became deeper,
the man gradually sank until the water reached his
neck. Endeavouring now to free his feet from the
mud, he found it impossible; for, with the weight

which he carried, he rolled over, sank, and was suffocated.

"Thus, from a miserly feeling, he would not follow the good advice given him by the king, and so lost his own life and the treasure which he carried.

"Now I advise you, Count Lucanor, let the sum be what it may, and the use of it here be ever so tempting, take care that avarice does not lead you astray, inducing you to risk your own life; for whoever should do so, setting his own life at small value, will certainly not receive the esteem of his fellowmen; unless, indeed, his honour is concerned thereby. For a man who sets small value upon his own life, and has not self-respect, cannot receive the respect of others. For it is certain that a man who properly respects himself will never risk his life through avarice or trifling causes, but only in defence of his honour."

And the Count, liking this advice, followed it. And Don Juan, admiring the precept, had it written in this book, and composed the following verses :—

> Who risks his life for greed of pelf
> Can hardly hope to enrich himself.

NOTE.

We believe this fable to be original, as we do not recollect having seen it in any collection. But, whatever may be its origin, or the changes that have been rung on it, the moral application which follows Patronio's recital assures to Don Manuel's production the most distinguished place

CHAPTER XXVIII.

Of what happened to a woman called Truhana.

OUNT LUCANOR once said to Pa-
tronio, "A man has unfolded to me a
scheme, and has shown me the manner
in which it can be carried out. And I
assure you that it is in so many ways admirable and
worthy of approval, that, if heaven blessed me with
the success it promises, it would be much to my
advantage; for so many things spring out of it, the
one from the other, that in the end it would be a
very great and noble achievement." He then informed Patronio of all the particulars. Who, after
he had heard the Count's arguments, answered him
thus :—

"My lord, I have always understood that it is
wisest to adhere to the things which are certain, and
not be ever running after shadows and vain things,
lest it happen to you as it did to Truhana."

The Count desired him to relate this story, which
Patronio did as follows :—

"A woman named Truhana, who was not very
rich, went one day to market, carrying on her head
a jar of honey. Along the road she was calculating
how she could sell the honey and buy eggs, these

eggs would produce chickens, and with the produce of the sale of these latter she would buy lambs; and in this way was calculating how she would become richer than her neighbours, and looked forward with anxiety to well marrying her sons and daughters, and how she would go through the streets, accompanied by her sons and daughters-in-law, and how the people would say what a fortunate woman she was to become so rich, having been so very poor. Under the influence of these pleasurable thoughts, she laughed heartily; when, suddenly striking the jar with her hand, it fell to the ground and was broken. Seeing this, she was in great grief at being so suddenly deprived of all her flattering anticipations; for, having fixed all her thoughts upon an illusion, she lost that which was real.

"And you, my lord, if you allow yourself to listen to everything that is proposed to you, so as to lose sight of the real and good, you can only blame yourself for your failure."

The Count was much pleased, and followed this good advice. And Don Juan, liking the moral, wrote, and ordered to be put in this book the following lines :—

> Confine your thoughts to what is real,
> And cease to nurse a vain ideal.

NOTES.

There is scarcely a language in which this fable does not appear under some form. It is, however, evidently of Eastern origin, as we find in the "Arabian Nights" a tale very similar —"Alnaschar, the Barber's Brother." The earliest version is in the fifth part of the *Pantcha Tantra*, entitled, "Aparickchita Kariteva," or, "Inconsiderate Conduct," the object of which is to show the danger of precipitation, and runs as follows:—

An avaricious brahmin, named Soma Sarma, had gathered, in charitable offerings, a large jar full of flour. On entering his home, he hung the jar upon a nail immediately opposite the foot of his bed, so as not to lose sight of it. During the night he awakened, and abandoned himself to the pleasurable reflections of gain, saying, "Now this jar of flour, in case of a scarcity, I can sell for at least one hundred pieces of money, and with this sum I can buy a ram and a goat; these will produce kids, and, selling these, I will purchase a couple of cows; after the sale of the calves I will procure a herd of buffaloes, which will turn out very advantageous and bring me considerable sums of money; then I shall have a stud, and will sell my horses to great advantage. I will build a fine house and become a man of consequence, when some rich and honourable man will give me his daughter in marriage, with a princely fortune. As I probably shall have a son I will call him by my own name, Soma Sarma; as soon as he can totter I will take him on horseback before me on the saddle, so that as soon as he sees me he will quit his mother's apron strings and come running towards me. I will call his mother to come and take him away from me: she, being occupied with the household affairs, will not attend to my summons, when I will give him a kick." Saying these words, he stretched out his foot so violently as to break the jar and upset all the flour about the place, where it mingled with the dust and was totally lost; and with it vanished the bright and flattering illusions of Soma Sarma.

The name of Truhana in the tale is equivalent to our Gertrude.

CHAPTER XXIX.

Of that which happened to a Man who was suffering from a malady and whose liver had to be cleansed.

ANOTHER time, Count Lucanor spoke thus to Patronio, saying, " Although God has been very bountiful to me in many ways, yet I am just now in great want of money ; and, although I would almost prefer dying to doing it, yet I feel I must be compelled to sell one of my estates, to which I am much attached, or have recourse to some other equally ruinous means to free myself from my present embarrassments. I am daily pressed by creditors who could well afford to wait. Now, knowing your good understanding, I pray you to tell me how I had best act under these pressing circumstances."

" My lord," said Patronio, " you are in much the same position with these men as the man was who was suffering from a malady."

" How was that ? " said the Count.

" Count," said Patronio, " a man was in great pain from a disease and was informed by the doctors that there was no other remedy than making an opening in his side and taking out his liver and washing it in certain medicated waters, as it was in a very bad state. While he was suffering under this operation, and the doctor held the liver in his hand, another man who was there demanded a piece of the liver for his cat.

"And you, Count Lucanor, if you desire to procure money at a serious injury to yourself to give to those who can afford to wait for it, you are certainly at liberty to do so if you wish, but you will never do it by my advice."

The Count, being very much pleased by what Patronio said, took care to profit by it; and Don Juan, liking the moral of the story, requested it should be written in this book, and composed these lines, which say as follows :—

> Know when to give and when withhold
> Or you may come to want untold.

CHAPTER XXX.

*Of what happened to a man who through poverty
and lack of other food, was reduced to eat some
peas.*

COUNT LUCANOR, speaking one day to Patronio, said, " God has been very bountiful to me, in granting me much more than I can individually enjoy; yet it sometimes happens that I am so pressed for

money, that my life is a burden to me. I beg of you
to direct me in this trouble."

"My lord," said Patronio, "in order that you
may better understand how to act under such circumstances, I will, with your permission, illustrate
your position by relating what happened to two rich
men."

The Count begged he would do so.

"My lord," said Patronio, "it is said that one of
these two men became so destitute that he could not
even procure bread to eat. After begging from door
to door, until wearied out, all he could procure was
a handful of dried peas, very hard and bitter. Remembering his former opulence, and seeing himself
now reduced through hunger to eat these peas, he
began to cry bitterly. As he ate he threw away the
pods, when he perceived another man behind him
eating them. And this is the point to which I
wish to draw your attention. When he saw the
man eating the pods, he asked him why he did so.
'Because,' said this latter, 'though I was once richer
than you ever were, yet I am now reduced to so
great a state of poverty and hunger that I am glad
to eat the pods which you are throwing away.'

"When the former man saw this, he found there
was yet another more destitute than himself, and less
deserving to be so. Seeing this, he directed his
heart to God and prayed that he might be shown
how to escape from so much poverty. His prayers
were heard, and he prospered ever after.

"And you, my lord, should know such is the world, and it is ordained that no condition admits of unalloyed happiness. If at any time, as it appears, you are distressed for money, do not let discontent enter your heart; but reflect how many men there are at the same moment, who have been both richer and more honoured than yourself, who would be only too glad to occupy what you consider an unfortunate position."

The Count was much pleased with what Patronio told him, exerted himself, and God helped him well out of his difficulties.

And Don Juan, liking the example, had it written in this book, and wrote the following lines :—

Let not poverty dismay your mind,
Since others poorer than yourself you find.

NOTES.

Without depriving the story of any part of its originality, we think the idea was taken from the "Gulistan," of Saadi, chapter the 19th, on the excellence of contentment. It also reminds us of an excellent Italian saying :—"A man is never so well as not to feel he can be better, nor so ill that he cannot be worse."

CHAPTER XXXI.

What happened to a Cock and a Fox.

AT another time Count Lucanor was conversing with Patronio, when he said, "You know, thanks be to God, my lands are very large, but are not all united, so that I have many places which are very strong and some which are not so—places which are separated a long way from the rest of my estate where my power is greatest. And, when I have any contention with the neighbouring nobles who are more powerful than myself, many who give themselves out for my friends, and others who volunteer their counsels, endeavour to terrify me on this score, and advise me on no account to go to those distant territories, and to keep within my own defences. Knowing your loyalty and superior judgment, I beg you to advise me how to act in this case."

"My lord," said Patronio, "it is difficult to advise in great and perilous undertakings, as no man can be certain of the results; for how often when we think we are acting for the best, things turn out unfortunately; while, again, what at another time appears to us the greatest misfortune, turns out to our best advantage. So a man, even with the best intentions, may give advice which may produce effects contrary to his previsions. If the advice is productive of no good, shame is his portion. In asking me to give you advice in so doubtful and perilous a position, I must beg you to allow me to relate to you what happened to a cock with a fox.

"My lord," said Patronio, "a good man had a house in the mountains, and among other things reared a great number of fowls.

"It happened upon one occasion, that a cock, wandering a long way from the house, met a fox, whom he no sooner observed than, fearing to become his prey, he flew up into a tree. The fox, seeing the cock in safety, felt very much annoyed at having missed his aim. He immediately began to consider how he could induce the cock to descend. He commenced by begging he would come down and continue his country walk. The cock abruptly refused him, when the fox, seeing he could not persuade him, began to threaten him, saying, that, as he could not trust him, he would find some means to catch him. The cock, finding himself in safety, laughed equally at his threats and promises. The fox, seeing that he could not intimidate the cock, began gnawing the tree and striking it with his tail. The captive cock, being frightened without reason, flew to another tree. The fox, seeing that he had alarmed him, continued pursuing him from tree to tree, each one taking him farther from home, until at last he caught him and eat him.

"And you, my lord, in your critical position, do
not let yourself be frightened at imaginary dangers,
but at the same time be prepared for real ones,
strengthening the defences of your smaller towns as
well as the large ones; and believe that no man
provided as you are with troops and provisions has
anything to fear behind his own walls. If through
uncalled-for fears you abandon your most distant
villages, they will chase you from one to another
until deprived of all. Even if you or yours show
the slightest disheartenment it will only serve to
strengthen your enemies, who, seeing your weakness, will never lay down their arms while you
possess an inch of land; but, if well defended from
the beginning, like the cock on the first tree, you
have nothing to fear from all the battering-rams and
scaling ladders of your enemies. Nay, more, to
convince you that I speak the truth, it would be
impossible to find an army sufficiently strong to
make breaches in, or undermine the walls of so
many fortified villages. But, my lord, when after
due consideration you have determined and commenced acting, on no account retract. It is always
better to face danger than to fly from it, more men
being lost in retreat than in the battle-field. Like
a little dog attacking a hound; so long as he remains
quiet, showing his teeth, he is safe, but once attempt
to run away and he is lost."

And the Count, feeling this to be good advice,
followed it, and was safe. And because Don Juan

thought this to be a good example, he had it written
in this book, and composed the following lines :—

> Defend thee like a man in proper season,
> But be not frighten'd when there is not reason.

NOTES.

This fable has nothing in common with that of La Fontaine
which bears the same title. In the Æsopian fable, versified by
the French poet, the cock does not fall a victim to the designs
of the fox. In Don Manuel's, on the contrary, he becomes,
after resisting all compliments, a prey to false alarms and want
of confidence when in actual safety. The moral which Don
Manuel intended to convey in his fable was not so much to guard
against the influence of flattery as against false alarms.

CHAPTER XXXII.

What happened to a Man catching Partridges.

COUNT LUCANOR, at another time
speaking to Patronio, said to him,
"Some men of high and low position
cause me and my people a great deal of
annoyance and injury, but, when appealed to, always
excuse themselves by expressing regret, and assuring
me that circumstances only compelled them to act in
the way they had done, and not their inclination.
Desiring to know how to act under these circumstances, I beg you to give me your advice."

"My lord," said Patronio, "in order that you

should know under these circumstances how best to act, I shall feel pleased at being permitted to relate ⸱ to you what happened to a man taking partridges.

"A man who had spread his net to take partridges, as soon as he had caught them, commenced killing them one by one, and, while so occupied, a gust of wind blew so fiercely in his eyes as to cause the tears to flow down his cheeks, when one of the birds that was still alive in the net said to the others, 'See, my friends, what pain it causes this good man to kill us, for you see it makes him weep.'

"Another partridge, more knowing, and who had avoided falling into the net, replied, 'My friend I am very thankful to God for having preserved me from falling into the snares of the fowler, and I will continue to implore Providence that I and my friends may be protected from all those who would injure us, excusing themselves by saying that they acted under the pressure of circumstances and against their inclinations.'

"And you, Count Lucanor, be on your guard against those you see are disposed to injure you under the plea that they are sorry for it. But if the damage be trifling, and evidently to you unintentional, and come from a person who has really been of service to you, I would advise you to shut your eyes and not notice it, unless you clearly see that he is taking an undue advantage of your good nature : it then becomes incumbent on you to defend your fortune and your honour."

The Count approved of this advice, and Don Juan, considering it a good example, ordered it to be inserted in this book, and wrote the following verses :—

> Who does thee ill and feigns regret,
> Beware of falling in his net.

And on this matter another verse was made by Alfonso, friar of Santiago, which says thus :—

> What avail the eyes that water
> If the hands are bent on slaughter.

NOTE.

The first germ of this fable appears in Indian collections : witness Lokman, fable 31. But Don Juan imparted to it an entirely new turn and form. The moral with which it winds up is essentially Spanish, and the advice given to Count Lucanor has every appearance of being addressed to the treacherous monarch Alfonso XI.

CHAPTER XXXIII.

Relates to what happened to a Man with his Friend who had invited him to dinner.

COUNT LUCANOR, when conversing one day with his counsellor Patronio, said, "A man came to me, proposing to carry out my views in a matter in which I am much interested, but the offer was made

with so little apparent eagerness that I am inclined
to think he would be glad not to be taken at his
word ; and although I am anxious to avail myself of
it, I am yet disinclined to accept a service so coldly
offered.   What do you think ?   Pray give me your
opinion."

"Then allow me, my lord," said Patronio, "to
narrate to you what happened to a man who had
been invited to dine with his friend.

"My lord, a man who had been very rich became
so reduced that he was often in want of the necessaries of life, which, however, he was too proud
to solicit, preferring to suffer the pangs of hunger to
the shame of begging his bread.   One day, however,
when very sorely pressed by hunger, having fasted
very long, he happened to pass the gate of an old
friend, who was at dinner, and who, seeing him go
by, invited him, but very coldly, to partake of his
repast.   The hungry man immediately accepted
the invitation, washed his hands, and sat down to
table, saying, ' Thanks, my friend ; you have invited
me in a lucky moment, and so generously that I
think it unbecoming to refuse you.'

"As the hungry man gained strength from the
repast he gradually lost the feeling of shame, and
God enlightened him as to the manner of freeing
him from his misery.

"And you, Count Lucanor, will now understand
how, as the offer is made and the service required,
you should accept your friend's proffered assistance

without hesitation, as it is always better to accept a favour if offered, than to ask one."

And the Count, following this good advice, profited thereby.

And Don Juan, liking the moral, composed these lines, to be written with it in this book, saying :—

> If thou have need, be not too nice ;
> Nor wait for friends to ask thee twice.

CHAPTER XXXIV.

What happened to the Owls and the Crows.

COUNT LUCANOR, conversing at another time with Patronio, said, " There is a man of considerable influence with whom I am at variance. This man had living with him a relation and his servant, to whom he was very kind. Lately some difference has arisen between this master and his servant; and the latter, considering himself ill-used, came to me, offering his services in my interests, if I would show him how he could be revenged. Having great confidence in your advice, I wish you to tell me how to act."

" In the first place," replied Patronio, " believe

me, this man seeks only to deceive you; and in
order that you may better understand how, I will
tell you what happened to the owls and the crows."

The Count begged him to do so, when Patronio,
continuing, said, "My lord, the crows and the owls
had a great contention, but the crows had the worst
of it; for the owls, whose custom it is to rove about
at night, and hide themselves in eaves during the
day, which made it difficult to find them, came in
the night to the trees where the crows lodged, killing
many of them and doing much injury.

"Suffering so much in this way, they consulted
an old crow who was very knowing, relating to him
the injurious treatment they received from the owls,
their enemies.

"He suggested to them this plan of revenge:
that they should pluck out of him all his feathers,
leaving only a few in his wings to enable him to fly
a little. In this sad state he went to show himself
to the owls, telling them that the crows had thus
cruelly treated him, merely because he wished to
make peace between them, and offered to show them
how they could be revenged on the crows.

"When the owls heard this they were much
pleased, and showed him much endearment, telling
him all their secrets and intentions. There was one
aged owl, however, who did not partake in the
general feeling. Seeing the deceitful intentions of
the crow, he told his companions not to trust him, as
he only sought to discover their secrets, and advised

them to turn him out of their society. But the owls, not putting faith in his advice, he left them, and sought for himself another hiding-place, where they could not find him.

"Thus the crow continued to live in confidence with the owls until his feathers were sufficiently grown to enable him to take a long flight. It was then he told the owls he wished to go and see where the crows were, in order that they might go with him and exterminate them. But he never returned until accompanied by all the other crows, whom he had informed of all the projects and hiding-places of the owls.

"In this way, the owls being attacked unprepared, and in the daylight, became easy victims to the vengeance of the crows; all through an unwise confidence in a natural enemy.

"And you, Count Lucanor, must know well that this man, being connected with the household of your enemy, will be naturally interested in its welfare. I would advise you to place no confidence in him, and if you do employ him, let it be only where no trust is required; for, be assured, he will deceive you and play you false the first opportunity favourable to his own interest, and so his proposed treachery to his present master will be turned against you."

The Count followed this advice, which was successful; and Don Juan, approving of it, had it written in this book, and composed the following lines :—

If thou wouldst live securely to the end,
Distrust a foe who would become a friend.

NOTES.

This example appears also to have had an Indian origin. It
is found in the third chapter of "Pantcha Tantra," under the
title of "Kàkoloûkika," or "The War between the Crows
and the Owls." Loiseleur des Longchamps, in his essay on
Indian fables, gives the following analysis of this tale :—
"The moral of this story is to show the danger of trusting to
strangers or enemies who come under the mask of friendship.
The king of the crows, jealous of the king of the owls, forms
the project of destroying his enemies, and to succeed more
securely therein, charges one of his ministers to introduce himself among the owls. He succeeds in his project by a ruse
which recalls the history of Zopyrus. Stripped of his plumes
and covered with blood, he is found, lying at the foot of a tree,
by the owls, who take him to their king. The new-comer
gains the confidence of the king of the owls, against the advice
of his ministers. He betrays their confidence, and shows
the crows how they can destroy their enemies, who are suffocated in the eaves which serve them as a hiding-place."

CHAPTER XXXV.

The advice which Patronio gave to Count Lucanor,
when he said he wished to enjoy himself, illustrated
by the example of that which happened to the
Ants.

OUNT LUCANOR, speaking one day
with Patronio, said to him, "Thanks
be to God, my friend, I am now rich
enough, and am advised by my friends
to give myself no more anxiety about the concerns
of this world, but, as I am in a position to do so,
to eat, drink, and enjoy myself; which I can do
without infringing on the interests of my children.
Having a high opinion of your judgment, I would
first seek your advice before acting."

"My lord," said Patronio, "although it is pleasant
enough to live for one's own enjoyment, yet it is first
advisable that you should hear what the ants did for
their own support."

"Willingly," said the Count.

"My lord, seeing what a little thing the ant is,
you might be led to suppose it is possessed of little understanding ; but remark, how in the harvest season
they quit their ant-hills, go to the fields, and return
laden with as much corn as they are able to carry,

which they deposit in their granaries, to be taken out when the first rain falls. It is supposed they do this to dry it, but that is not the case, as the ants also take the corn out at the beginning of winter, when there is little or no sun to dry it. But were they to take it out every time it rained their labour would be incessant. The reason why they bring out their corn after the first rain is that they find it begin to grow, when it would take up so much room in their granaries that, instead of supporting, it would suffocate them. So they eat the dry grain, leaving the other to ferment outside; and, knowing that this fermentation lasts only a short time, they have no fear in doing so of losing their provisions. Nevertheless, during all this time, they do not cease adding to their stores, either from a dislike to idleness, or an unwillingness to despise the gifts of Providence.

" And how can you, Count Lucanor—seeing the prudent foresight and economy displayed by the little ant, in providing for his own wants—charged, as you are, with the care of a large property, and responsible for the well-being of so many of your fellow-creatures, think only of living in idleness and ease, which shows a littleness of spirit; forgetting also, that by constant expenditure, with no regard to the augmentation of your means, you must ultimately bring yourself to ruin ? My advice to you is, enjoy yourself as much as you like, but do not do so at the expense of your honour and fortune. Be you ever so rich, you will never lack occasions to increase the lustre of your name and enhance the happiness of your fellow-men."

The Count was much pleased with the advice given by Patronio, and acted upon it.

And as Don Juan found this also a good example, he ordered it to be written in this book, with these lines :—

> Let not thy lavish hand expend thy hard-earned gains,
> Live so that honour'd life and death reward thy pains.

NOTES.

The advice which Don Manuel gives us in his fable, when he introduces the ants, is more noble than that of La Fontaine, in whose fables we find three examples where the ant is introduced. The one most resembling Don Manuel's is "The Ant and the Grasshopper," indeed this is an exact transcript in verse of Æsop's fable bearing the same name, both inculcating industry, and reproving a life of sensuality and pleasure.

The industry and foresight of the ant have been alluded to by the great Eastern philosopher in the following well-known passage :— "Go to the ant, thou sluggard; consider her ways, and be wise. Which having no guide, overseer, or ruler, provideth her meat in the summer, and gathereth her food in the harvest."—Proverbs of Solomon vi. 6-8.

CHAPTER XXXVI.

*Of that which happened to a good Man and his Son,
who boasted of having many Friends.*

SPEAKING again, on another occasion,
Count Lucanor said to Patronio, "I
have, as you know, many friends.
Well, they give me to understand that
they are all most sincerely devoted to my interests,
and that, happen what may, nothing shall induce
them to desert me. Now tell me, I pray you, what
is your opinion as to how far I may depend upon
their sincerity and trust them?"

"My lord," said Patronio, "good friends are the
best things this world has to give. I always, however, feel some doubt of the sincerity of him who
makes great professions, and wait for an opportunity
to prove the value of his declarations. But that you
may know how to judge a real friend, hear, I pray
you, what happened to a good man and his son, who
told him he had many friends."

"Willingly," said the Count.

"My lord, a good man had a son, whom he
advised, among other things, to always endeavour
to make many good friends.

"In compliance with this advice, he liberally

dispensed his goods amongst many men, with the view of cultivating their friendship, and these vowed to him their readiness to risk their souls and bodies in his service.

"One day the father inquired of the son how he progressed in the cultivation of his friendships.

"'I have many friends,' replied the son, 'and amongst them I am certain of ten who would lay down their lives in my service, and who now only want an opportunity to prove their sincerity.'

"The father marvelled much at this, and could not conceive how his son, in so short a time, had made so many and such friends; for, in the course of his long life, he had never been able to make more than one friend and a half.

"The son did not like his father's questioning the truth of his statement, and insisted that what he said was true.

"'Try them, then,' said the father, 'and in this manner. Kill a pig and put it into a sack, and carry it to the house of one of these friends, telling him it is a man you have slain, that you are in great dread of its being discovered, and, as it is quite certain that neither you nor those in any way cognisant of the fact can escape the death which awaits such a deed, beseech him, as a friend, to conceal the bad action, and, if need be, to help you in your defence.'

"In this way the son did as the father suggested, visiting each friend in turn. All alike told him that, under any other circumstances, they were willing to make any sacrifice for him, but in this case they were afraid to venture, and besought him for the love of God to tell no one he had been to their house. Some went so far as to tell him they should never help him more, but they would pray for him; others said they would not forsake him on the scaffold, and would procure him honourable burial

"When the young man had thus proved his friends, and could find none to assist him, he returned to his father and told him what had happened.

"'You now see,' said the father, 'that those who have lived longest know best how difficult it is to procure a sincere friend. As I said to you before, I have only one friend and a half; go, try this last.'

"The young man did so. Arriving at the house of this half-friend late at night, carrying the dead pig on his shoulders, he knocked at the door, and told him of his misfortunes, and how he had been treated by his friends, begging of him for the love he bore his father to help him.

"The half-friend told him that, although between them there existed neither love nor friendship, yet, for his father's sake he would conceal him. He then took the sack carefully from the shoulders of the son, thinking it contained a dead man, and conveyed it into his garden, where he buried it amongst the cabbages, carefully arranging them afterwards, and then sent away the young man contented.

"When this latter came home to his father, he related all that had happened.

"'So far good,' said the father; 'now when next you meet this man dispute with him so as to lead to a quarrel, then strike him a blow on the face.'

"This the young man did; and when he had struck the blow, the half-friend said, 'My son, you act badly; nevertheless, I shall never reveal the secret which is between us.'

"And when the young man told this to his father he sent him to try his other friend. When he arrived at the house of his friend, and had told him, as before, all that had happened, he promised to guard him from death and danger.

"Now it came to pass that about this time a man had in reality been killed in the city, but no one knew by whom, and as the young man had been noticed going about at night, carrying a loaded sack, he was immediately suspected, judged, and sentenced to death. The friend of his father, seeing no possibility of his escape, determined to sacrifice his own son in the stead of his friend's, and went to the judge, saying he knew the prisoner was not guilty, as it was his own and only son who committed the deed—the son acknowledging what the father had said, and thus, by his own death, saving the life of the son of his father's friend.

"And now, Count Lucanor, having told you how friends are proved, I hold this for a good example to find out who are indeed your friends, and how to know if they will risk danger in your defence. There may be many good friends, 'but there are many who cannot be depended upon in adversity, for friends too often only grow with good fortune.

" Again, this example may be taken in a spiritual sense, in this manner :—although men may think they have many friends, yet, when on the point of death they are often destined to see the vanity of worldly friendship in the professions of friends, who say that they are willing but cannot help them ; and of the clergy, who can only say they will pray to God for them. The wife and children may express their readiness to go with them to the tomb, or promise a sumptuous interment ; nevertheless, none aid them to escape death, as did the son of the good man, who gave his life to save his friend. The dying man finds he must turn to God as his only resource.

" Now the sinner, seeing he cannot escape the death of his soul, unless he turns to God, who—like a merciful Father and true Friend, remembering the love which He bears to man, the work of His hands —like the good friend, sent His own Son, Christ Jesus, to suffer and die, He being innocent, to redeem sinful man. So did Jesus, like an obedient son, do His Father's will. He, being true God and true Man, sought and suffered death, and redeemed sinners by His blood.

" And now, Count Lucanor, it is desirable that you reflect and find out which of these friends is best and truest, and whose friendship is most worthy of confidence."

The Count was much moved by this exhortation, and acted with advantage upon its suggestions.

And Don Juan, liking so good an example, caused it to be written in this book, and composed the following lines :—

> Never can man find out a friend so good
> As God, who sought to save him by His blood.

NOTES.

This graphically written tale, which is intended to show the difficulty of acquiring a true friend, is of early date, its invention not being due to Don Manuel. There is but little doubt of its being of Arabic or eastern origin. We first find it in a work entitled, "Disciplina Clericalis," written by Pedro Alfonso, who originally was a converted Jewish rabbi named Moses Sephardi, born in the year 1062, at Huesca, in the kingdom of Arragon. He was a man of much learning; and at the age of forty-four embraced Christianity, when he was appointed by Alphonso XV., king of Castile and Leon, physician to his palace. The tale alluded to in this work is the "Lesson given by a Father to his Son," and commences, "Arabs moriturus,"—"An Arab dying." We find some of the fables from this "Disciplina Clericalis" in the "Arabian Nights;" indeed, this narrative, in various forms, has been translated into all languages. The French have many versions of this tale; it has been published in Germany, in the "Imitations of Oriental Tales," by Herder; and we see it in Boccaccio, the tenth day, eighth novel.

The scarcity of true friends, a truth so generally accepted, is noticed in an old collection of Greek fables, where a friend of Socrates remonstrating with him for building so small a house, the philosopher replied that, "Little as it is, he were a happy man that had but true friends enough to fill it." The allusions made by our English writers to pretended friendships are too well known to render any mention of them necessary, yet I cannot but remark that it forms the subject of one of Gay's best fables, "The Hare with many Friends."

CHAPTER XXXVII.

Relates to what happened to the Lion and the Bull.

AT another time, when Count Lucanor was conversing with Patronio, he said to him, "Patronio, I have a very powerful and honourable friend, of whom, up to this time, I have never had occasion to complain; but now, from various circumstances which have occurred, it is clear to me that he is not so well-disposed towards me as before, and he appears to be seeking for an opportunity to quarrel with me, from whence I see two causes of uneasiness : the one is, that if he openly declares himself my enemy it will cause me serious injury; the other is, if he suspects that I mistrust him he will in turn lose confidence in me, and thus, this feeling increasing by degrees, will bring about an open rupture. Knowing your great prudence and foresight, I beg of you to advise me how to act under these circumstances."

"My lord," said Patronio, "that you know how to protect yourself I have no doubt; I shall tell you, however, what happened to the lion and the bull, to illustrate your present situation.

"The lion and the bull were very great friends; being both powerful and strong they lorded it over all the other animals; so the lion, with the help of the bull, drove off all carnivorous animals, and the bull, with the aid of the lion, drove away all other animals that ate grass.

"The animals, seeing how the combined influence of the lion and the bull caused them so much injury, consulted together how best to free themselves from this strait. With that view they resolved to cause, if possible, some ill-feeling or want of trust between them; and, knowing that the fox and the sheep were most in the confidence of their enemies, desired to bring them over to their cause, succeeding in which, the fox, who was the lion's counsellor, commenced by telling the bear that he was the strongest of all the carnivorous animals after the lion, and induced him to insinuate to the lion that the bull was playing him false, assuring him that he had spoken something unfavourable of him some few days since. The sheep also, who was the adviser of the bull, induced the horse, the most powerful of all graminivorous animals after the bull, to cause the bull to doubt the friendship of the lion.

"Now neither the bull nor the lion believed exactly what the bear and the horse had told them, although they were ranked next to themselves, yet the mutual confidence which previously existed was shaken, they became more distant, trusting more to their respective counsellors; which the other animals seeing, spoke out more boldly, and said the lion and the bull were jealous of each other, and felt in their hearts unfriendly.

"Now the fox and the sheep, thinking only of their own interests and future safety, took no trouble to undeceive their lords, so that the love and friendship which previously existed between them turned to distrust and hatred. The other animals, seeing this, united together to increase the ill-feeling which now existed between the lion and the bull. The result in the end was, that they found themselves deprived of the power which they enjoyed when united, and were subjected to the insults of the combined animals, who, now acting together, would not allow themselves to be again subjected to the dominion of their former lords, who found out, but too late, that they were the victims of calumny.

"And you, my lord, take care, that those who would create in your mind suspicions against your friends do not lead you into trouble, as did the animals the lion and the bull. Now I would advise you, if you have always found your friend loyal and true, to trust in him as you would in a good son or brother. Shut your eyes to trifling circumstances, for, be assured, if he intends doing you a serious injury, you will always see some indications of it beforehand. If your friend be merely a time-server, carefully avoid giving him cause to believe that you suspect him; but, if once you find that his dishonourable intentions admit of no doubt, then, instead of quarrelling with him, endeavour first to persuade him not to desert you and forfeit your friendship—endeavour to convince him that mutual harmony is essential to the well-being of both. By these means, and by not allowing yourself to be led away by false representations, you will avoid falling into the error of the lion and the bull."

The Count was well pleased with what Patronio had related. And Don Juan, approving of this example, caused it to be inscribed in this book, and composed the following lines :—

> To lying slanders ne'er attend
> Against a tried and proven friend.

NOTES.

This apologue, like many others written at the same period, has not only a general but also a political moral. It warns us against losing our friends by the misrepresentations of others, as also it cautions those in power against that treason and perfidy which would divide them from their allies and most sincere dependants.

"This tale is very ancient; it is found in the Sanscrit work "Pantcha Tantra," the first chapter of which is entitled "Mitra-Bhèda," or "The Rupture of Friendship." The personages of this Indian apologue figure as the king lion, *Pingalaca*; the bull and his friend, *Sandjivaca*. The confidants of the lion and the bull are two jackals, named *Carataca* and *Damanaca*. In this case, the two jackals, jealous of the friendship existing between the lion and the bull, unite, and, by misrepresentations, endeavour to destroy this amity. Differing from Don Manuel's tale this results only in the death of the favourite by his master.

CHAPTER XXXVIII.

Relates to the advice which Patronio gave to Count Lucanor, when he expressed a desire to obtain a good reputation; and the example was what happened to a Philosopher who was suffering from a severe illness.

"PATRONIO," said Count Lucanor, "the thing a man should most desire to acquire in this world is a good reputation, and, having gained it, to be ever watchful, lest it be sullied by any act of his own or others. As I know that no one can counsel me better than you, I beg of you to advise how best to increase and guard my good name."

"My lord," said Patronio, "it will afford me great pleasure to give you my opinion, and illustrate it by what happened to an aged philosopher."

The Count expressing a desire to know what that was, Patronio commenced by saying, "A well-known philosopher lived once in a town in the kingdom of Morocco, who suffered from an ailment affecting his sight. His physicians forbade his leaving the house, and ordered him not to expose his eyes too much to the light.

"One day, however, thinking his sight sufficiently restored, he ventured to walk alone into the town, where he had many disciples, but the glare of day so increased his defect of vision that he accidentally strayed into a narrow street close at hand, and which happened to be one inhabited by most disreputable characters, of which fact he was not aware; but, being seen issuing therefrom by some of his friends and disciples, he was immediately suspected of having belied in a moment all his former virtuous life and professions.

"So it is that men occupying certain positions are judged without pity, their slightest failings being criticised; whilst others, whose position calls for but little attention, appear to escape notice, although guilty of much greater errors. So it was with the philosopher, against whom a general outcry was raised. When he arrived at his house, he was waited upon by many of his disciples, who in great grief demanded why he should have so sacrificed his former reputation, bringing scandal on himself and them likewise.

"When the philosopher heard this he was

astounded, and demanded to know what evil he had done, and where.

"They replied that he had been publicly seen to leave the street occupied only by disreputable people.

"When the philosopher heard this he was in great trouble, and said to his disciples, 'Do not be uneasy; I will give you an answer in eight days.' And, shutting himself up in his study, he composed a very good and useful little book, in the form of questions and answers between him and two of his disciples, on good and bad fortune. 'My sons,' said he, 'good fortune often comes to us unsought as well as sought, and, unfortunately, the world is too apt to judge from the result of an action, being unconscious of the motive which guided it; so also we find men without ability or energy blessed by good fortune undeserved; whilst others, more really meritorious, meet only with misfortune. Again, disasters are not always of our own seeking, as a man may, in the street, unintentionally have his head broken by a stone thrown at a bird: this accident is not of his own seeking, but the result of ill chance. Know, my sons, both in good and ill fortune two things are necessary; the one is, that we should thank God for the good we have received and the evil we have been enabled to avoid, the other is that rarely or never does any good action pass without its reward, as evil deeds also bear their penalty. Again, we should ever pray to God to deliver us from evil and false judgment, as happened to me the other day, when, through the infirmity of a bodily ailment, I, without harm in thought or deed, unknowingly entered a street of ill fame, and thereby forfeited my good reputation.'

"And you, Count Lucanor, in order to increase and perpetuate your reputation, three things are essential; firstly, let your good actions be done solely with the motive of pleasing God, regardless of the opinion of mankind, keeping unsullied your honour and position, seeking not fame undeserved by good works; secondly, pray to God to strengthen you, and inspire you to perform such good actions and from a motive so pure as will even gain for you the esteem of all good men; thirdly, never by word or deed, give cause for a shadow of suspicion to rest on you, as the world is too apt to misconstrue and misjudge the best intentions. Still, ever remember that the only infallible judge of your actions is God and your own conscience."

The Count thought this good advice, and prayed to God to help him so to act as to save his soul and increase his honour.

And Don Juan, finding it a good example, had it written in this book, and made the following lines :—

Let all thy acts be clear of blame,
That slander breathe not on thy fame

CHAPTER XXXIX.

Of what happened to a man who was made Governor
of a large territory.

OUNT LUCANOR, speaking another
time with Patronio, said, "Patronio,
many tell me that, being very powerful
and much honoured, there now only
remains for me one thing which is most essential,
and that is to acquire riches. And, as I know that
you have always advised me for the best, and that
you will still continue to do so, I beg of you to tell
me what is most incumbent on me."

"My lord," said Patronio, "the advice which you
require of me demands grave consideration, for
two reasons. Firstly, that my ideas may be apparently contrary to your interest ; and, secondly, it is
difficult for me to give advice having the semblance
of indifference. Nevertheless, as all loyal advice is
meant only to benefit those to whom it is given, I
will tell you honestly and without flattery what I
think, seeking only your well-being. Now there is
much truth and much falsehood in what has been
told you ; to convince you of which I have only to
relate what happened to a man who had been made
governor of a large territory."

The Count asked him what that was.

" My lord," replied Patronio, "it was customary in a certain territory to elect every year a governor, who, during the twelve months that his command lasted, was implicitly obeyed, and treated with all due reverence; but, at the expiration of the year, he was deprived of his command, position, and everything, even to his clothes, and left to perish in a desolate island. It once happened that a man who was so appointed, having more foresight and a clearer understanding, and knowing that they would treat him in the same manner as his predecessors, prepared beforehand for what he knew would inevitably happen. During the year of his supreme command, he ordered a house to be secretly built on the island where he knew he was to be placed, and had it furnished and provisioned so as to leave him in no want of the comforts and necessaries of life, and arranged with his friends and relations that they should send him anything he might have forgotten. When the year of his command was completed and he was left, like the previous governors, naked to perish on the island, he quietly sought his secret abode, where he lived to enjoy the advantage of his precautions.

" And you, Count Lucanor, if you wish to be well-advised, remember that you are not destined to live here for ever; the day will assuredly arrive when you must leave this world naked as you came into it, taking nothing with you; all that remains to you are the good or bad deeds you may have performed.   Take care, therefore, so to act as to procure for your soul a happy abode in the kingdom where life is counted not by years, but is everlasting; remembering that your soul is not mortal, and can never perish, and that your good or evil actions in this world will be rewarded or punished in the next according to their deserts.   I advise you, therefore, never to forget that power, honour, and riches are perishable, and how unwise it is to sacrifice to them the certainty of eternal life.   And again, seek not to exalt yourself by publishing your good works before men.   At the same time, let your actions be such as to deserve the prayers of your friends, when you are no longer able to intercede for yourself.   Yet, when you have duly provided for the future happiness of your soul, when your duties here on earth are accomplished, you may look for the promotion of your honour and prosperity in this world."

And the Count, finding this very good advice, prayed to God to help him to put it into practice.

And Don Juan, approving of it also, caused it to be inscribed in this book, and composed the following verses :—

> In quest of this world's fleeting pleasure,
> Lose not the more enduring treasure.

NOTES.

We find in the "Imitations of Oriental Tales," by Herder, a similar story to the above, called, "The Desert Island," but the religious allegory is not reproduced in the German work. This beautiful production remains a monument to the Spanish moralist who has succeeded in raising this fable and some others to the rank of an evangelical parable.

Herder's version of "The Cid," which was long a bone of contention among critics—some saying he had naturalised these grand old ballads into German, others that he had distorted and disfigured them—has lately been discovered to be a literal translation of a French prose version.

CHAPTER XL.

Of that which happened to Good and Evil, illustrated by what occurred to a Man with a Madman.

NE day Count Lucanor said to Patronio, " I happen to have two neighbours ; one is a man whom I love very much, and with whom I have much sympathy ; nevertheless, he does things at times which cause me much annoyance. Now, with the other man, I have no friendship, although I have often occasion to be grateful to him. This latter also at times, by his proceedings, gives me some trouble. Now, will you advise me, with your usual good sense, how to manage these two men ? "

" Count Lucanor," said Patronio, " what you tell

me is not one thing alone, but two things—one being very distinct from the other; and I will, with your permission, exemplify to you, by two narratives, how .you should act under these circumstances."

The Count agreeing to this, Patronio said as follows :—

"Good and Evil agreed once to live together, and Evil, who was soon found to be cunning and rebellious, always seeking some deception or mischief, proposed to Good to purchase a flock of sheep wherewith to maintain themselves. Good, being naturally peaceable and accommodating, agreed. When the sheep had brought forth their young, Evil proposed to Good to shear them ; to this, the latter, not agreeing, requested Evil to act upon his own responsibility. Now, as Evil is always ill-disposed and seeking mischief, this sanction pleased him very much, so he proposed to Good to retain for his share the young lambkins and rear them, whilst he, Evil, would reserve for himself the milk and the wool of the sheep. To this Good assented without complaining. Evil now proposed that they should rear pigs. To this Good agreed as before. This time Evil, pretending to great ideas of justice, proposed that as Good had on a former occasion taken the young lambkins, and he, Evil, the wool and milk of the sheep, they should this time reverse it, he now taking the little pigs, and Good the milk and wool.

"Again, Evil proposed that they should have a kitchen-garden, in which they cultivated turnips; when these had come to perfection, Evil said to Good, as it was difficult to judge the value of what could not be seen, that Good should take the leaves and he would be contented with what was buried in the earth; and so he did. Again, they planted cabbages, and, when these had grown, Evil said to Good that in justice Good should take this time what was under the earth, and he would take what appeared above it.

"Now Evil thought it would be convenient to have a woman for their household service, and, Good agreeing with him, Evil proposed that Good should have for his share of the servant from the waist upwards, that being the superior and most useful part of the body, whilst he, Evil, would content himself with the inferior half, or, from the waist downwards. Good, who desired nothing better than the help of two strong arms for the work of the house, was perfectly satisfied with this arrangement, but, as the woman thus became the wife of Evil, she had a son. Now, when she wished to nourish her child, Good resolutely opposed her doing so, saying, that the milk belonged to him.

"When Evil found he had a son he was much pleased, but, on hearing the child cry very much, inquired of the woman why it was so uneasy. To which she replied that it was for want of nourishment; and, hearing this, Evil told her to give the child the food it required. But she said to him that Good had strictly forbidden her to do so, as the milk belonged to him, it being his share.

"Now Evil went to Good and told him he should insist on having the milk given to his son. To which Good simply replied that, as the milk belonged to his share, he would never consent.

"Hearing this, Evil became incensed, and Good, seeing him in this great strait, quietly answered, 'My friend, surely you did not believe me so foolish as not to have seen how cunningly and for your own exclusive interest you have heretofore divided matters between us. You never considered my wants or necessities, so you should not now feel any surprise that when you require my assistance I am unwilling to grant it. This will serve to remind you of all you made me suffer.'

"Now, whether it was that Evil felt the truth of what Good had said, or that he feared to lose his son through hunger, he prayed of Good that, for the love of God, he would take compassion on the innocent child, and not condemn him to suffer thus for his father's faults, promising that henceforward he would always do all Good should require of him; and Good, hearing this, praised God, who in His mercy had thus permitted him to bring good out of evil, and replied to Evil that he would agree to the woman's nourishing the child, on condition that the father should take the child in his arms, and go through the streets of the city, and proclaim

aloud that Good had conquered Evil without departing from the paths of virtue.

"To this Evil consented, too glad, at any sacrifice, to be able to save the life of his son; and
hence we know that good has ever conquered evil
with good.

"But it happened otherwise with the good man
and the madman. Now it chanced that a good
man kept some baths, and a neighbour, a madman,
was the first to come daily to this bath; afterwards
awaiting the arrival of the people to bathe, he commenced, as soon as he saw them, to beat them with
sticks or throw stones at them, so that the pro-
prietor of the baths soon lost all his customers.
The good man, seeing this, determined to rise very
early one day, undressed himself, and went into the
bath before the madman arrived, having at hand a
pail full of very hot water and a wooden club.
When the madman came to the bath, determined,
as usual, to attack all who came in his way, the
good man, seeing him enter, allowed him to approach, when he suddenly upset the pail of hot
water over his head, attacking him at the same time
with the club. The madman now gave himself up
for dead; nevertheless, he managed to escape, and,
running away, he told everyone he met to be careful, for there was a madman in the bath.

"And you, Count Lucanor, since chance has
given you two neighbours who may occasionally
abuse your friendship, yet be friendly with them;

heed not their small faults, and give them to understand you seek not revenge, but desire to act kindly
towards them, helping them in their necessities,
showing them that, though you need not their good
services, yet you desii : their friendship and esteem,
not as an obligation but through good will."

The Count, liking this advice, followed it with
success.   And Don Juan, taking this to be a good
example, ordered it to be written in this book, and
composed the following lines :—

> The evil man must be withstood,
> Till evil be o'ercome with good.

NOTE.

Don Manuel, in illustrating, as we see in this apologue, that
good arises out of evil, had a more enlightened and philosophical
view of the subject than he was probably aware of.

In this chapter we have two examples, but La Fontaine, who
was only acquainted with the first part, as he found it in Rabelais,
has made the former the subject of one of his least commendable
tales.   Had he been able to read Don Manuel's apologue in its
integrity, he would doubtless have constructed from it a fable
more edifying.

CHAPTER XLI.

Of the association between Truth and Falsehood.

OUNT LUCANOR, speaking with Patronio, said to him as follows :—

"Know, Patronio, that I am in great trouble and confusion, in consequence of some men who, having no regard for me, take every opportunity, by treachery and lying, to injure my reputation, never failing, at the same time, to turn these lies to their own advantage. It is true I could retaliate upon them in the same manner, but I have such a hatred of deception and lying that I cannot allow myself to adopt the same line of conduct, I beg, therefore, you will advise me how best to deal with these men."

"Count Lucanor," said Patronio, "Falsehood and Truth once entered into an agreement to keep company together. After a time Falsehood proposed to Truth that they should plant a tree, so that when it was very hot they might enjoy the shade thereof, to which Truth, being always straightforward, agreed. As soon as the tree had taken root and begun to show signs of life, Falsehood proposed to Truth that, to avoid disputation each should take a portion of the tree as his own; Falsehood at the same time, suggesting that Truth should take the root, giving as a reason with much colouring and argument, that it was the most desirable part; 'For,' said he, 'it is well protected by the earth, while the part out of the ground is liable to be damaged and even destroyed by evil-disposed men cutting it down, to be gnawed by beasts, or injured by birds with their claws and beaks; the great heat may dry it up, or the frost destroy it, but from all these dangers the root is protected.'

"When Truth heard all these reasons, being confiding by nature, and believing all she heard to be true, she accepted the offer made by Falsehood, thanking him for his consideration.

"Falsehood was greatly pleased at the success of his deception and coloured representations.

"Truth, having accepted the root of the tree as her portion, had to reside there, under the earth; while Falsehood remained above, taking up his abode amongst men and things, where he prospered.

"The tree began to grow, throwing out branches well covered with leaves and flowers of brilliant and attractive colours, giving altogether a most delightful shade and protection from the heat. When the people saw this they sought the shade of the tree of Falsehood, so that it became the resort of all the idle and others from the villages round, who sought its protection, and were there taught by Falsehood the art of deception and untruthfulness. In this manner, he taught some the art of telling the lie simple, as making promises, saying, 'Dear sir, I will do so and so, never intending, at the same time, to do it. To others, the lie double, as swearing homage and promise of service, knowing at the time that they are uttering a falsehood, and practising deception. Also the lie malicious, which is the most fatal of all, as it is falsehood and deceit under the colour of truth. In this art Falsehood was very learned, and so skilfully did he convey his instruction to all those who took shelter under his tree, that there was scarcely a man who was not an adept in this art; so attractive, indeed, was this to the people, either from the beauty of the tree or the protection which it afforded, that nearly every one became subservient to this master, so that, in the end, people who were really honest scarcely dared to speak the truth or esteem themselves.

" Now Falsehood, finding himself so flattered and honoured, began to despise Truth, who still remained hidden under the earth, so that no man living knew where to find her, or thought of seeking for her.

" Truth, finding in the end that she had nothing but the roots of the tree apportioned to her by Falsehood, began gnawing and tearing them; and although the tree had, as before mentioned, fine branches, luxuriant foliage, and brilliant flowers— affording a grateful shade, with every promise—still it perished without bearing fruit, from Truth eating the root thereof.

"One day, when Falsehood and his disciples

13   .

were quietly reposing beneath the shade of his tree, a gust of wind blew it down, the root thereof being destroyed, and, falling on Falsehood, it seriously injured him, besides wounding many of his companions. It was then that Truth issued from her subterranean abode, and standing by the wreck of the fallen tree, proclaimed aloud how all the treachery of Falsehood had only tended, as they saw, to his own destruction.

"And you, Count Lucanor, observe well that falsehood, like the tree, has wide-spreading branches, with its flowers, representing its sayings, its thoughts, its deceptive pleasures, enticing many under its shade, waiting for the fruit which never comes to perfection, and, if perchance it should, is never enjoyed. Now, if your enemies make use of the deceptive wisdom of falsehood, your only alternative is to be on your guard against them. Never be led to be one of their companions in this art, envy not their apparent success, which can only end in disgrace and discomfort to themselves. Flattering as it may appear, it will end, like the tree of falsehood, in the destruction of those who seek its protection ; and, although truth may be despised and hidden for a time, yet esteem her, and attach yourself to her as the only good whereby you can succeed in this world and obtain salvation and the grace of God in the other."

Count Lucanor was much pleased with the advice which Patronio gave him, and acted upon it.

Don Juan, liking the example, had it written in this book, and made the following verses :—

Adhere to truth, from falsehood fly;
For evil follows all who lie.

CHAPTER XLII.

Of what happened to a Fox who pretended to be dead.

COUNT LUCANOR, upon another occasion, sought the advice of Patronio, informing him that he had a relation in a distant land, whose possessions were so very small that he could scarcely defend himself against his more powerful neighbours, " who, feeling their superiority, leave no means untried to vex and annoy him ; and he is so wearied of this daily suffering, that he is willing, at any cost, to free himself therefrom. I, too, am anxious to see him at ease."

To which Patronio replied : " My lord, in order that you may best know how to advise your relation in this serious difficulty, allow me to relate to you what happened to a fox who feigned death.

"A fox one night entered a hen-house, and, after causing much destruction amongst the fowls, found, when he was about to return to cover, that it was already daylight and that the people were about.

Seeing that he could no longer conceal himself, he furtively went into the street, where he lay down, feigning death.

"When the people saw him lying there apparently dead they paid no attention to him, until a man who passed shortly after, observing, as he thought, a dead fox, remarked that hair from the forehead of a fox was an excellent remedy against convulsions in children. So, taking out his scissors he clipped some hair from the forehead of the fox. Others, passing by, had a notion that the fur from the back and loins of a fox was good in some other complaint, and so on, until they nearly deprived him of all his fur. Still, the fox never moved, feeling that his loss was comparatively trifling. Others came, saying that the nails of a fox's foot were an infallible remedy against sudden fear, and tore them off. Still the fox gave no signs of life. Another, believing a fox's tooth to be a cure for the toothache, drew one of his teeth. At last a man came, saying a fox's heart was infallible in heart disease, and took out his knife to cut out the fox's heart, which the animal perceiving, and knowing that he should now lose his life if he delayed, resolved, no matter at what risk, to endeavour to save himself; and he succeeded and escaped.

"And you, Count Lucanor, will, by this example, see how you should advise your friend not to heed slight infringements, but to let them pass by unnoticed, unless, indeed, his honour is impugned. A man

need never blush at not being as strong as his neighbours, so long as he is contented. He only need
feel shame who knows not how to suffer or to resist;
but, when there is real danger, then he should risk
everything in defence of his right and honour, for
this is of greater value than life itself."

And the Count approved of this advice. Don
Juan, also considering this a good example, desired
that it should be written in this book, and composed
the following verses :—

> The ills that touch not life contented bear;
> Avoid the rest with utmost skill and care.

NOTES.

Don Manuel anticipated by some few years the archpriest of
Hita, in whose poems we find the above tale recited (see Sanchez,
"Poesias anteriores al Siglo, xv." 1795). The details, however,
differ from Don Manuel in some respects, insomuch as that it is a
cobbler who cuts off the tail of the fox to make a pair of soft
shoes, or some such thing. Then a surgeon takes away a part of
his jaw, as a cure for the toothache; an old woman then deprives
him of an eye, to cure the pallor of young girls; a doctor next
cuts off his ear, as a remedy for ear complaints. The fox, however, in the same manner as told by Don Manuel, preserves his
life by a resolute escape.

CHAPTER XLIII.

What happened to two blind Men travelling together.

AT another time when Count Lucanor was conversing with his friend Patronio, he said to him, "I have a relation in whom I have great confidence, and I am certain that he is much attached to me. Now he wishes me to undertake an expedition with him. I am myself by no means desirous of joining him, as I have doubts of its success; but he assures me I have nothing to fear, and that he would rather suffer death than that I should receive any injury. I beg, therefore, you will give me your opinion as to my proceeding."

"My lord," said Patronio, "for this purpose it is desirable you should hear what happened to two blind men travelling together."

The Count desiring to know what that was, Patronio continued as follows:—

"A blind man, who lived in a city, was, upon one occasion, visited by a man likewise blind, who proposed that they should both go to a neighbouring town, and endeavour to maintain themselves by charity, when the other remarked that the road was so hilly and dangerous that he feared to go.

"'But,' replied the other, 'have no fear, for I will go with you and take care of you,' pointing out to him, at the same time, so many advantages that would accrue from going there, that he trusted in his companion, and they both went.

"It was not long after they had arrived at the dangerous part of the road, when the blind man who led the way fell, bringing down with him his companion who had feared to undertake the journey.

"And you, Count Lucanor, if your fears are well founded, and the expedition is really dangerous, do not allow your friend to persuade you to join in the undertaking, for his dying for you would, under misfortune, benefit you nothing."

The Count followed the advice with advantage, and Don Juan, thinking well of the example, had it written in this book, and composed the following couplet to be placed at the end :—

Be not induced to take a false direction
By promises of safeguard or protection.

NOTES.

This narrative may be considered as founded on the wise parable of Jesus, wherein He said to His disciples, "Can the blind lead the blind ? shall they not both fall into the ditch ?" This same precaution to avoid being led physically by incapable, or morally by designing persons, to the ruin of your estate here or your salvation hereafter, has been proverbialized by all nations.

CHAPTER XLIV.

Of what happened to a young Man on his Wedding Day.

NE day Count Lucanor was talking to Patronio his counsellor, and said to him, "Patronio, one of my dependants tells me he can make a very advantageous marriage with a woman much richer and more honourable than himself; but there is one difficulty in the way, which is this, he tells me he has been informed that she is of a very violent and impetuous temper. Now I beg you to counsel me whether I should allow him to marry this woman, knowing such to be her disposition, or whether I should forbid it."

"Count Lucanor," replied Patronio, "if the man is like the son of a good man, a Moor, advise the marriage by all means; but if such be not the case, forbid it."

The Count begged of him to relate the narrative.

"There lived in a city," said Patronio, "a Moor who was much respected, and who had a son, the most promising youth in the world; but, not being rich enough to accomplish the great deeds which he felt in his heart equal to, he was greatly troubled, having the will and not the power.

"Now in the same town there lived another Moor, who held a higher position, and was very much richer than his father, and who had an only daughter, the very reverse in character and appearance of the young man, she being of so very violent a temper that no one could be found willing to marry such a virago.

"One day the young man came to his father, and said, 'You know that your means will not allow you to put me in a position to live honourably,' adding that, as he desired to live an easy and quiet life, he thought it better to seek to enrich himself by an advantageous marriage, or to leave that part of the country.

"The father told him that he would be very happy if he could succeed in such a union. On this, the son proposed, if it were agreeable to his father, to seek the daughter of their neighbour in marriage. Hearing this, the father was much astonished, and asked how he could think of such a thing, when he knew that no man, however poor, could be induced to marry her.

"Nevertheless, the son insisted; and, although the father thought it a strange whim, in the end he gave his consent. The good man then visited his neighbour, telling him the wish of his son.

"When the good man heard what his friend said, he answered, 'By heaven, my friend, were I to do

such a thing I should prove myself a very false friend,
for you have a worthy son, and it would be base in
me to consent to his injury or death; and I know
for certain that, were he to live with my daughter,
he would soon die, or death, at least, would be pre-
ferable to life. Do not think I say this from any
objection to your alliance, for I should only be too
grateful to any man who would take her out of my
house.'

"The young man's father was much pleased at
this, as his son was so intent on the marriage. All
being ultimately arranged, they were in the end
married, and the bride taken home, according to the
Moorish fashion, to the house of her husband, and
left to supper; the friends and relations returning to
their respective homes, waiting anxiously for the
following day, when they feared to find the bridegroom either dead or seriously injured.

"Now, being left alone, the young couple sat down
to supper, when the bridegroom, looking behind
him, saw his mastiff and said to him, 'Bring me
water wherewith to wash my hands.' The dog,
naturally taking no notice of this command, the
young man became irritated, and ordered the animal
more angrily to bring him water for his hands,
which the latter not heeding, the young man arose
in a great rage, and, drawing his sword, commenced
a savage attack on the dog, who, to avoid him
ran away; but, finding no retreat, jumped on the
table, then to the fireplace, his master still pursuing

him, who, having caught him, first cut off his head,
then his paws, hewing him to pieces, covering
everything with blood. Thus furious and blood-
stained, he returned to the table, and, looking round,
saw a cat. 'Bring me water for my hands,' said
he to him. The animal not noticing the command, the master cried out, 'How, false traitor, did
you not see how I treated the mastiff for disobey-
ing me? if you do not do as I tell you this instant
you shall share his fate.' The poor little harm-
less cat continuing motionless, the master seized
him by the paws and dashed him to pieces against
the wall. His fury increasing, he again placed
himself at the table, looking about on all sides as
if for something to attack next. His wife, seeing
this, and supposing he had lost his senses, held her
peace. At length he espied his horse, the only one
he had, and called to him fiercely to bring him
water to wash his hands. The animal not obeying,
he cried out in a rage, 'How is this? Think
you that because you are the only horse I have that
you dare thus to disobey my orders? Know then
that your fate shall be the same as the others, and
that anyone living who dares to disobey me shall
not escape my vengeance.' Saying this, he seized
the horse, cut off his head, and hacked him to
pieces.

"And when the wife saw this, and knowing he
had no other horse, felt that he was really in earnest,
she became dreadfully alarmed.

"He again sat down to table, raging and all bloody as he was, swearing he would kill a thousand horses, or even men or women, if they dared to disobey him. Holding at the same time his bloody sword in his hand, he looked around with glaring eyes until, fixing them on his wife, he ordered her to bring him water to wash his hands.

"The wife, expecting no other fate than to be cut to pieces if she demurred, immediately arose and brought him the water.

"'Ha! thank God you have done so,' said he, 'otherwise, I am so irritated by these senseless brutes that I should have done by you as by them.' He afterwards commanded her to help him to meat. She complied; but he told her, in a fearful tone of voice, to beware, as he felt as if he was going mad.

"Thus passed the night; she not daring to speak, but strictly obeying all his orders. After letting her sleep for a short time, he said to her, 'Get up, I have been so annoyed that I cannot sleep; take care that nothing disturbs me, and in the meanwhile prepare me a good and substantial meal.'

"While it was yet early the following morning, the fathers, mothers, and other relatives came stealthily to the door of the young people, and, hearing no movement, feared the bridegroom was either dead or wounded; and, seeing the bride approach the door alone, were still more alarmed.

"She, seeing them, went cautiously and tremblingly towards them, and exclaimed: 'Traitors,

what are you doing ?   How dare you approach this
gate ?   Speak not—be silent, or all of us, you as
well as I, are dead.'

" When they heard this they were much astonished,
and, on learning what had taken place the night
previous, they esteemed the young man very much
who had made so good a commencement in the
management of his household; and from that day
forward his wife became tractable and complaisant,
so that they led a very happy life.

"A few days later, his father-in-law, wishing to
follow the example of his son, likewise killed a horse
in order to intimidate his wife, but she said to him,
' My friend, it is too late to begin now ; it would not
avail you to kill a hundred horses : we know each
other too well.'

" And you, Count Lucanor, if your dependant
wishes to marry such a woman, if he be like this
young man, advise him that he may do it with safety,
for he will know how to rule his house : but if he be
not likely to act with resolute determination at the
beginning, and to sustain his position in his household, advise him to have nothing to do with her.   As
also I would counsel you in all cases where you have
dealings with men to act with that decision which
will leave them no room to think that you can be
imposed upon."

The Count thought this a very good example,
and Don Juan had it written in this book, and
made these lines, saying :—

Who would not for life be a henpeck'd fool
Must show, from the first, that he means to rule.

NOTES.

A translation of the above story, by Mr. F. W. Cosens, was separately printed a short time since, and was copied into the *Athæneum* of June 29, 1867, with some preliminary remarks calling attention to its remarkable resemblance in general idea to the "Taming of the Shrew"—a resemblance which Ticknor was the first to point out in 1848 ("History of Spanish Literature," vol. i. p. 66), and which had escaped the notice of all the Shakespearian editors and commentators.

As the Editio Princeps of "El Conde Lucanor" was published at Madrid in 1575, it is, of course, possible that Shakespeare may have seen the book, or, if not, that he may have heard the story from one of the wits and poets of Elizabeth's court.

In a French work, entitled, "La Collection de Legrand D'Aussy," will be found a similar tale to Don Manuel's— "La Dame qui fût corrigée," where the same remedies are employed, but with greater brutality, as the husband, not content with killing his dogs and his horse, beats his wife and knocks out the eye of a disobedient servant. Again, we find the same subject in two Italian works; one is in the fourth volume "Novelliero Italiano," which has been prettily arranged for the French stage, under the title of "La Jeune Femme Colère;" and again, there is the same tale found in the "Notti Piacevole di Straparola." Two brothers, having married two sisters, on leaving the church for their respective homes, one brother presented his wife with a pair of trowsers and two sticks, proposing to her that she should decide which was to be master. She immediately acknowledged his superior right. He then led her to the stables, under the pretext of showing her his horses, and, finding one that was restive, beat him and killed him. The wife profiting by this example, the husband had ever after only to extol her mildness and obedience. The other began very differently; being too much in love with his wife, he allowed her to gain a complete ascendency over him, and thus caused his misery. At length he went to consult his brother, who informed him of what he had done. On returning home, this foolish husband led his wife to the stable, and killed a horse in her presence; he then offered her the trowsers and two sticks, requesting her to choose, but she laughed at him; so that he only lost a horse for his pains.

From the resemblance of this and the like tales to Don Manuel's account of "What happened to a Young Man on his Wedding Day," written in the fourteenth century, it is pretty clear that he was the originator of the idea.

CHAPTER XLV.

Of what happened to a Merchant who went to buy Brains.

NE day Count Lucanor said, "Patronio, I am furious at a thing I have been told, as it tends greatly to my dishonour; and I fear it will provoke me to act with so much rashness and impetuosity as may cause a scandal."

Patronio, seeing the Count so irritated, said to him, "My lord, permit me to relate to you what happened to a trader who went one day to buy brains."

The Count assenting, Patronio continued as follows:—

"My lord, there lived in a town a famous master, whose sole business was to sell brains. One day the trader of whom I spoke went to this man who sold brains, saying that he wished to become a purchaser.

"The other replied he was very willing to serve him; but desired to know what price he would go to, as the quality would be according to the price he was disposed to pay for it.

"The trader offered him a maravedi,* which he took, saying, 'My friend, when you are invited to a dinner, and know not the number of dishes of which it is composed, eat heartily of the first which is presented to you.'

"The trader replied that was very poor value for his money; to which the other said, 'As I told you, it is according to the price given.

"The trader then presented him with a dollar; and the other told him that, when he should find himself in a rage never to act on the impulse of his feelings, but to wait until he had well considered all the circumstances. The trader, finding that, at this rate, he would be expending many dollars, resolved henceforward to seek advice in his own brain, for better or for worse.

---

* A Spanish copper coin, thirty-four of which make a real de vellon, which is about threepence English.

" Now it happened that this trader, having occasion to go to a distant country by sea, had to leave
his wife while she was with child. More than
twenty years passed without any tidings of him.
The mother, having a son, and believing her husband
to be dead, she having no other child, continued to
eat and sleep with her son, as had been her custom
from his birth ; she, from her great love for her
husband and child, calling the boy her husband. It
now happened that the trader, having completed his
business, turned towards home with his fortune, and
arriving at the gate of the city where he lived, passed
on without making himself known to anybody, and
quietly sought his own house, where he concealed
himself that he might see what was passing.

" Now when it was evening and the young man
came home, the good wife said, 'Good husband,
whence come you ? '

" The trader, hearing her call this young man her
husband, was much grieved, not because she had
married him, but, seeing so young a man, he feared
she was leading an immoral life. He determined at
once upon killing her, but, recollecting the advice
which had cost him a dollar, kept cool. By-and-bye
they sat down to table, which the trader seeing, felt
still more irritated, but he yet remembered the
advice he had received, and would not allow himself
to be carried away by his passion ; but, when night
came, and he saw them lie down together, he felt it
impossible longer to restrain his anger, and issued

from his hiding-place, intending to kill them; but, suddenly remembering the brains which he had purchased, became quiet.

"Now, before the fire was quite extinguished, the woman commenced crying bitterly, 'O, my son and husband, I hear that a vessel has arrived from the country your father journeyed to; for the love of God, I pray you to go early in the morning, and perchance you may hear some news of him.'

"The trader, hearing this, and remembering the situation in which he had left his wife, concluded this might be his own son, and felt much pleased, thanking God very heartily that he had not killed him as he intended; and now thought the dollar which he had expended in the purchase of brains well laid out, as it had taught him self-command.

"And you, Count Lucanor, do not act hastily and before you have given yourself time to ascertain the truth and certainty of that which you complain of; but, once satisfied on this point, let not anger carry you away, or influence you to do anything which may hereafter give you cause for repentance.

The Count was pleased with this advice, and followed it. Don Juan, approving of this example, ordered it to be written in this book, with the following lines :—

> If your anger hastily you vent,
> 'Twill be your fate at leisure to repent.

NOTES.

How much unhappiness would be spared in this world if the advice given in the two lines appended to this amusing tale were more strictly followed. How unwise is it to act while under the influence of a passion which tramples beneath its feet all guardian agencies; how much better to give some time to reflection, as Norfolk advises Buckingham, when he says, "Stay, my lord, and let your reason with your choler question what 'tis you go about" —*Henry VIII.*

It is well often to take counsel of our pillow, or, as the Italians say, in a beautiful proverb, "La notte è la madre di pensieri,"— "Night is the mother of thoughts." Neither should it ever be forgotten that we may some day be reconciled to the person who now excites our passion, and live to regret the too hasty utterance of observations which may ever mar that unity of feeling which previously existed, for, as the Spaniards say, "Amigo quebrado y soldado mas nunca sano,"—"Broken friendships may be soldered, but never made sound."

So far concerns the moral. The narrative, however, throughout is novel and full of point, showing that good brains, like any other article, should or ought to bring to the vendor a value proportionate to their worth.

CHAPTER XLVI.

What happened to a Man with a grey Sand-piper and a Swallow.

N another occasion, Count Lucanor, speaking with Patronio, said, "Patronio, in no way can I escape having a quarrel with one of my two neighbours. It happens that one of these is nearer to me than the other ; I beg you, therefore, to advise me what to do under these circumstances."

"My lord," said Patronio, "that I may the better do this, allow me to relate what happened to a man with a sand-piper and a swallow."

"Willingly," replied the Count.

"There was a feeble old man who was so annoyed by the chirping and chattering of the sand-pipers and swallows which surrounded his dwelling, that he begged a friend to get rid of them for him, as he found they entirely prevented his getting any rest.

"His friend replied that he was willing to comply with his request, but that it would be impossible to get rid of both of them at the same time. It therefore only remained for him to decide which should be removed.

"To this the old man replied that the swallows

made the most noise, and were the greatest nuisance; 'But, you know,' he says, 'the swallows go and come; I should therefore, prefer getting rid of the sand-pipers, as they are always stationary.'

"And you, Count Lucanor, although your more distant neighbour may be the more powerful, I would advise you rather to quarrel with him than with your adjoining one, although he be the weaker."

The Count liked this advice, and followed it with much benefit.

And Don Juan, thinking it to be a good example, ordered it to be written in this book, and composed the following lines :—

> If thou be forced all ways to exchange a blow,
> Choose the more distant, though more powerful foe.

NOTES.

This fable teaches us the well-known maxim, "Of two evils choose the less," a question often requiring the exercise of our best discrimination. And, if an enemy must exist, there can be no question that a distant one is more to be tolerated than the endless annoyance of a nearer one; the more so, when broils and offences were, in Don Manuel's time, more frequently decided by the sword than by an appeal to justice.

The sand-piper (*Totanus*) alluded to chiefly frequents the sands and shingly shores of the sea coast. It is a noisy bird, and utters shrill and wailing cries.

CHAPTER XLVII.

What happened to the Devil, with a Woman who went on a Pilgrimage.

OUNT LUCANOR, conversing one day with Patronio, his counsellor, said, "Patronio, I and some other persons were talking together lately, and inquiring in what manner a bad man could inflict most evil upon others and make them suffer most. Some said, by rebellion; others, by evil-doing; and some declared that the thing of all others which made a man most dangerous was an evil and slanderous tongue. Now, as you have so good an understanding, I pray you to tell me from which of these injuries the persons suffering from them would be likely to receive most harm."

"My lord," said Patronio, "that you may the better understand my opinion on this matter, I should like to relate to you what happened to the Devil, with a woman who went on a pilgrimage."

The Count, requesting to hear the narrative, Patronio proceeded as follows:—

"In a certain town there resided a young man of good personal appearance and his wife, who lived so happily together that they were never known to disagree. The Devil, seeing this, and always going about seeking to do evil, was much grieved at this semblance of worldly felicity, and determined to leave no means untried by which he could mar their happiness and draw them into his meshes.

"One day he was returning from the town where this couple lived, sad and dejected at the ill-success of his schemes, when he met an evil-disposed woman in the guise of a pilgrim. Having saluted each other, she asked him from whence he came so sad. He told her he was returning from the town where the man and woman lived, detailed their state of happiness, and how he had been going about for some time to cause dissension between them, but without success.

"She said she was much astonished, and the more so, knowing his cunning, at his being frustrated; and so promised, if he would follow her advice, she would soon put an end to his troubles.

"The Devil consented to do all she suggested, provided she could cause a difference between the man and his wife. They immediately made arrangements for their future operations.

"The woman then went to the town where the young couple resided, and devoted the whole of her time to watching their habits and proceedings. She ultimately called at their house, saying that she had been an old servant in the family and was anxious, if they would engage her to devote her whole life to their service.

"The good wife, believing in her word, unfortunately took her into her house, and confided to her, after a while, all her secrets, as did also her husband.

"Now, after living in their service for some time, and becoming the confidant of both parties, she came one day, with a sad face, saying to the wife, 'I fear from what I have seen that your husband is devoting himself more to another woman than he ought, and I come to advise you to lose no opportunity in securing his love by a more devoted attention—the loss of his affection being the greatest evil that could happen to you.'

"When the good woman heard this, although she could scarcely believe it, yet it had the effect of making her anxious and sad.

"The false servant seeing this, then went to meet the husband, who she knew was returning home from a certain place, and, with a woful face, told him that, much as she disliked it, she felt it her duty to inform him that she feared his wife loved another more than himself; at the same time praying, for the love of God, he would not tell his wife, or she would kill her.

"The young husband, hearing this, would not believe it; nevertheless, it had the effect of causing him to be very depressed and dejected.

"The woman, seeing this, hastened home to the wife, saying to her, with great feeling, 'My dear child, I cannot understand how it is that your husband is becoming so indifferent to you; and, that you may believe in my fidelity, take notice when he comes in how angry and sad he is, contrary to his usual custom.' On leaving the wife she went to the husband with the same story.

"As soon as the husband reached the house, and found his wife so dejected and so different from her usual appearance, he became more uneasy. After a while the servant proposed to the wife to consult some soothsayer, who could advise her the best method of regaining and securing her husband's affection. The wife, who desired to again live happily with her husband, willingly assented to this. In a few days the servant informed her mistress that she had found a wise man, whom they now consulted, and who gave her to understand that, if she cut a few hairs from her husband's beard, under the chin, it would have the effect of instantly removing all his anger, and they would live in harmony, as before, and perhaps more happily; at the same time giving a razor for the purpose. The young wife, anxious to regain her husband's former love, and again live happily as before, consented to do as suggested.

"The false servant now turned to the husband, telling him that she was miserable at the prospect of losing him, but she could no longer conceal it from him that his wife intended to kill him and go away with her admirer; adding that he might verify the truth of her statements. She now said that his wife and her lover had arranged to kill him in the following manner. She then suggested that he should come in by-and-bye to take a little rest, and told him that, as soon as he was asleep, his wife intended cutting his throat with a razor.

"The husband was much alarmed at what the woman told him, resolving inwardly to test the truth of her assertion, guarding himself by precautions from any actual danger. On returning home, his wife received him more kindly than she had done for some time, asking him why he so incessantly worked, taking so little rest; inviting him, at the same time, to lie down and place his head on her knees while she lulled him to sleep.

"On the husband's hearing this he felt convinced of the truth of the servant's statement, and, in order to test his wife's conduct he lay down as she proposed, resting his head on her lap, and in a little time feigned to be asleep. She now took in her hand the razor to cut off the hairs from his throat, as advised by the false servant; when the husband, surprising her with the razor in her hand in the act of applying it to his throat, no longer doubted her treachery, and, starting up with alarm, seized the razor from her hands, and instantly decapitated her. The wife's father and brothers, hearing the noise which this struggle occasioned, ran hastily into the room and were horrified at the spectacle they there beheld, and, having never heard any evil reports against the young woman, immediately attacked the young man and slew him.

"Again, the relatives of the young man, hearing

how unfairly he had been slain, attacked in their turn the father and brothers of the wife, and killed them. This brought others into the fray, so that many in the town lost their lives.

"All this was caused by the false representations of the wicked servant; but, as God never permits evil, known or concealed, to go unpunished, so it was soon discovered that all these misfortunes arose from the hypocrisy and false representations of a deceitful female pilgrim, who, being brought to justice, was condemned to a most cruel death.

"And you, Count Lucanor, if you desire to know what class of men are most dangerous in society, learn, from this recital, that they are those who, under the guise of friendship or otherwise, introduce calumny and false representations for the destruction of good feeling. I advise you, therefore, to be most on your guard against *religious cats* or 'sanctimonious traitors,' against whom the Scriptures also caution us, saying, 'A fructibus eorum cognoscetis eos,'—'By their fruits ye shall know them.' For certain it is that no man can long conceal entirely his thoughts and intentions; there will arise occasions when they will escape him and attract attention."

The Count found much truth in what Patronio had said, and prayed to God to preserve him and his friends from the baneful influence of all calumniators.

And Don Juan, liking the example, had it written

in this book, and composed the following lines, which say :—

> The doings, not the semblance, heed,
> Wouldst thou from evil chance be freed.

NOTE.

We are strongly inclined to believe that Molière, in writing his celebrated "Tartuffe," had in view the fable of Don Manuel. Although the characters introduced are not exactly alike, yet his severe criticisms on the hypocrisy of the abbés of his day (so generally commented on at that time by most writers) resemble in that and in the construction of the story the little drama of Don Manuel, wherein is so vividly depicted the great evil of hypocrisy, and where, by misrepresentations, not only is the happiness of one family destroyed, but several murders committed, and, indeed, a whole town involved in a general massacre.

In this tale I have not translated literally the invitation made by the wife, "Y que ella lo espulgaria," fearing it might be offensive to the eyes of some of our readers. In making this remark, I cannot but comment on the general refinement of Don Manuel's writings, and their entire freedom from the grossness which, at a later period, characterized the works of some of the best Spanish writers.

CHAPTER XLVIII.

The advice which Patronio gave to Count Lucanor when informed that a Man had offered to teach him the art of foretelling coming events, which he exemplified by what happened to a good man, who became first rich and afterwards poor, by the intervention of the Devil.

NE day Count Lucanor said to Patronio, "A man tells me that he knows many ways and signs whereby to foretell coming events, which art he desires to teach me, so that I may be enabled to increase my power and better my possessions. But, as my conscience inspires me with the feeling that this is not altogether without sin, before I accept his offer, I wish you to direct me what to do."

"My lord," said Patronio, "in order to illustrate your situation, allow me to relate to you the story of the man with the Devil."

"Willingly," said the Count.

Patronio proceeded as follows :—"A very rich man arrived at such a state of poverty that he was unable to maintain himself, which misfortune made him very wretched. One day, being particularly sad, and wandering alone among the mountains, he chanced to meet the Devil, who, though from his intuitive knowledge he was well aware of what was passing in the man's mind, nevertheless asked him why he was so sad.

"The man replied, it was no use telling him, as he could not remove the cause.

"The Devil answered, and said to the man, that, if he were willing to comply with all he required of him, he would prove to him that he was able to relieve him, and that he knew why he was unhappy. He then related all that had happened to him and the cause of his sadness, asking him again if he would accept his conditions, as, if so, he would relieve him from his misery, making him richer than any of his family had ever been before, saying that he was the Devil, and had the power to do it.

"The man, hearing this, felt a little alarm; nevertheless, his misery was so great that he ultimately agreed, on condition of being made very rich, to do all that was required of him.

"So it is that the Devil always knows his time to make men fall into his snares. When he sees us in any trouble or necessity, it is then that he offers us his assistance to avoid labour and anxiety for the sake of an immediate apparent relief. So it was that he obtained possession of this man, making him his slave.

"The conditions being arranged, the Devil told the man that he must now become a robber, and

that he would give him the power to open the gate
or door of any house he desired, no matter how
well secured it might be; and if by chance he were
taken prisoner, he had only to cry out, 'Help me,
Don Martin,' and he would come and set him free
from all danger.

"On these conditions, the man set out for the
house of a rich merchant, under the cover of night
(for evil-doers always avoid the light). He reached
the door, which the Devil opened for him; and it
happened in the same manner with others, so that in
a short time the man found himself very rich indeed,
and lost all remembrance of his former poverty;
but, not content with his riches, he still continued
his career of robbery, until, being caught at last
and taken to prison, he called on Don Martin, who,
speedily arriving, placed him at liberty. Nevertheless, he yet continued his former practices, and being
taken prisoner, he called, as before, for his deliverer,
whose attendance was not so prompt as on the
former occasion. When he asked him how he
dared to deceive him, and why he delayed so long
in coming to help him, the Devil replied that he was
particularly engaged at the moment. He was again,
however, liberated.

"Now the man, seeing the facility which which he
was freed from prison, still continued his robberies,
but, Don Martin not responding to his last appeal,
he was tried and sentenced to die. After sentence
was passed, Don Martin once more placed him at

liberty in the name of the king. Again this man
returned to his old courses, and again was taken
prisoner. This time, however, Don Martin did
not arrive until he was at the foot of the scaffold.
The man then told Don Martin this was no
child's-play, for his delay had caused him dreadful
alarm.

"Don Martin replied he had brought him five-
hundred maravedi in an alms-bag, which he was to
offer to the judge, who would immediately liberate
him. Now, while they were making preparations,
there appeared some difficulty in procuring a rope,
when the man, calling the judge aside, gave him the
bag containing the money.

"The judge, after a short time, turning to the
people, said, 'My friends, did you ever see a rope
wanting when the man is really guilty? it is clear
that God does not desire the death of the innocent;
therefore we shall defer the execution until to-
morrow. Examine his antecedents more carefully,
and, depend upon it, justice shall be satisfied.' This
the judge did to gain time to count the money in
the bag, where, instead of money, finding only a
rope, he immediately ordered the execution of the
prisoner, who, having the rope round his neck,
called again on Don Martin, who attending, he
desired to know why he had deserted him in this
extremity; to which the Devil replied that, under
any circumstances he could help him, except when
he had a rope round his neck, as then he—the

Devil—was deprived by this of his power. The consequence was that the culprit met the fate which awaited him, losing thereby both soul and body, from not resisting the temptation of the Devil; such being the fate of all those who rely upon false aid and delay their repentance. And, if you doubt my word, think of what happened to Alvar Nuñez and Garcilaso, who were most credulous men and believed in all manner of signs and prognostications.

"And you, Count Lucanor, if you desire to save both soul and body, put your trust and hope in God, who will never desert you, and not in omens and predictions; for it is a great sin to doubt the power of God, placing your hopes on auguries and such occult fancies."

And the Count, thinking this good advice, followed it with much benefit. Don Juan also considered it so good an example as to be worthy of being written in this book, and he composed the following lines :—

> Who doth not trust in God repose,
> Evil his life and sad its close.

NOTES.

The study of astrology, witchcraft, or demonology, and the occult sciences, occupied much attention at the period when Don Manuel wrote, and he, fearing not to be wiser than his time, has chosen in the above tale an example entirely in conformity with the opinion he desired to propagate. The Devil he shows us as the first of all sorcerers, and makes him powerful only for evil. We see, however, in all the old writers who had faith in sorcery, that, while admitting the agency of evil, there yet remained a doubt as to its fulfilment, consequent upon the permission of an all-superintending superior agency of good. This same drama we see enacted in the present day, in the form of pantomime, where the efforts of the evil one are ultimately rendered abortive by the watchful spirit of goodness. There is a very old fable in Sir Roger L'Estrange's collection, which is curiously like the one above, where a malefactor who had committed I know not how many villanies and run through the discipline of many jails, made a friend of the Devil to help him out of all his distresses. This friend of his brought him off many and many a time, and still he was taken up; again and again he had recourse to the same Devil for succour. But, upon his last summons, the Devil came to him with a great bag full of old shoes on his back, and told him plainly, "Friend," says he, "I am at the end of my line, and can help you no longer. I have beat the hoof till I have worn out all these shoes in your service, and not one penny left me to buy more, so that you must e'en excuse me if I drop you here."

CHAPTER XLIX.

What happened to Don Lorenzo Xuares Gallinato,
when he beheaded the renegade Priest.

COUNT LUCANOR, speaking one day with Patronio, said to him, "A man came to me recently offering his services. I know him to be a good man, nevertheless I have heard so many tales about him that I am undecided as to accepting his offers. Now, as I know your ability to give me good advice, I beg you to tell me what I should do in this affair."

"Count Lucanor," said Patronio, "in order that you may know how best to act in this affair, allow me to relate to you what happened to Don Lorenzo Xuares Gallinato."

The Count desiring to know what that was, Patronio spoke as follows :—

"Don Lorenzo Xuares Gallinato lived a long time in the service of the King of Granada, and when it pleased God to restore him to the favour of the holy King Ferdinand, this latter asked Don Lorenzo one day how he ever hoped for mercy and salvation, having so long served the Moors against the Christians.

"Don Lorenzo replied that he thought he had

never done anything very offensive to God, unless it was that he once had killed a priest.

" King Ferdinand, thinking this a very grievous sin, asked him how it happened : to which he replied that, being in the service of the King of Granada, who trusted everything to him, and being an officer of the body-guard, he one day accompanied the king, on horseback, to the city, where they heard in a street a riotous noise, as if made by many people.   On putting spurs to his horse and advancing to ascertain the cause of the tumult, he found a Christian priest surrounded by people to whom he declared his intention to become a mussulman and deliver over to them the God in whom the Christians believed and trusted.   This unhappy traitor, having procured vestments and raised an altar, celebrated mass thereon, and, after consecrating the sacred Host, delivered it over to the people, who commenced its desecration by dragging it through the streets and treating it with every mark of opprobrium.   Seeing this, he, although living among the Moors, remembering he was a Christian, and firmly believing the dogma of his faith, and that what they were insulting was the body of Christ Jesus who had died for the redemption of sinners, thought this was a happy occasion to risk his own life to save from further insult the sacred Host, and revenge those outrages which had been already offered to it ; so, descending from his horse, drew his sword and slew the offending priest.   He then knelt down in adoration before God who had been so insulted. At this the Moors became outrageous, attacking him with sticks and stones, and causing a great uproar, which the king hearing, rode forward to inquire the cause, finding Lorenzo, sword in hand, defending himself against the Moors, who sought to kill him. He called upon the people to desist, at the same time inquiring the cause of the disturbance, which the Moors related to him with great anger, and how Don Lorenzo had killed the priest. The king demanded to know how he had dared to do so without orders; when Don Lorenzo simply answered that he was a Christian, and that, as the king trusted the care of his person to him, his loyalty and duty would ever compel him to suffer death rather than that the sacred person of his majesty should be insulted, so his duty as a Christian obliged him to sacrifice his life in defence of the sacred body of the King of kings and Lord of lords; if his majesty desired to punish him for this, he was ready to submit to his commands. The king, hearing this, understanding his motives, and knowing his fidelity, appreciated him and loved him more.

"And you, Count Lucanor, if you know this man is really trustworthy, heed not what is said against him, but act as the King of Granada did towards Don Lorenzo Xuares Gallinato; but, if you think the man deceives you and is unworthy of your confidence, avoid accepting his offer of service."

The Count was much pleased with the advice which Patronio had given him. And Don Juan, liking the example, had it written in this book, and wrote the following couplet :—

Many things unreasonable seem,
Which, when better known, we find deserve esteem.

NOTES.

This chapter is wanting in the early editions of "Count Lucanor," and the void is explained by the defective state of the manuscript apparently used by Argote de Molina, which is that supposed to have come from the convent of Peñafiel, to which it was bequeathed by the author. Fortunately, another manuscript has been discovered in the National Library of Madrid, containing the whole of the fable, which is given in the excellent edition of Don Pascual de Gayangos (Madrid, 1860).

CHAPTER L.

Concerning that which happened to Saladin and a Lady, wife of a Knight in his service.

COUNT LUCANOR spoke to Patronio one day in the following manner :—

"Patronio, I know for certain that you have an excellent understanding, and that there is no man on earth better able to give advice in any case than you ; I pray you, therefore, to tell me what, in your opinion, is the best qualification a man can possess. I am more needful of your opinion because I am conscious how many qualities a man requires to enable him to act well and with success ; for a man may have a good understanding, and, nevertheless, not act well. Such being the case, I desire to know the one thing most essential for me to remember and cherish under all circumstances."

"My lord," said Patronio, "I thank you for your praise, but more especially for the honour you do me in appreciating my understanding. Nevertheless, I fear you may err in this particular, knowing as I well do, how easy it is to deceive ourselves in our judgment of mankind, as we have to determine two things : the one, what is the disposition of a man ;

and the other, what is his understanding. Now, to
clearly know what is a man's real character we must
see how he acts towards God, as also what is his
conduct towards the world; for, much as he may
aypear to do good works, and allowing that he
really may perform some good and worthy actions,
yet these may be directed only to his greater advantage in this world; so that all this specious virtue
and merit, which certainly serves its purpose for
the day, will be found void of all solid foundation,
and will not exempt a man from the suffering
consequent upon sin.

"Now others perform their good works for the
service of God only, regarding not the world. We
all know this is the better part, being that which
will secure for us eternal happiness in the future;
nevertheless, those who elect either the one or the
other extreme should consider well the course they
are pursuing—the one acts and lives only for this
world, the other is quite regardless thereof.

"Now, as man owes a duty both to God and to
the world, he should so regulate his conduct as to
perform good actions, guided by purity of intention
in all things—a task almost as difficult to accomplish
as to hold his hand in the fire without feeling the .
heat.

"It is, therefore, right that a man should, in all
his actions, consider that he owes a united duty to
God and man, for there have been many good kings
and holy men who have fulfilled these two duties.

"Again, to judge a man's understanding, requires us to weigh well his good works. Many men are found with good solid sense, who cannot at the same time speak two sentences correctly; whilst others act perfectly, if you believe their own recital and description of what they do and intend doing; nevertheless, their deeds are of small value.

"How is it, then, that men act so well in their own opinion and so contrariwise according to the ideas of others? like to those whom the Scripture calls fools—running about with drawn swords in their hands, always ready to destroy all who contradict them; or, as princes who abuse their might and power.

"Now, that you may be able to judge which man is most pleasing to God and the world, who possesses a real good understanding, whose intentions are pure, and whose words deserve credence, you must carefully judge them by their works; and this must not be done hastily and without due consideration, but you must cautiously watch, even if for a considerable period, in order to ascertain if prudence, justice, a kind regard for the feelings of others, and a true spirit of charity guide their words and deeds.

"I have entered into a consideration of the motives which should and do influence men, particularly as you have paid me so honourable a compliment, which, perhaps, after a mature consideration, you might not feel inclined hastily to repeat, in order that you may decide for yourself which is the qualification most essential and most beneficial to man; and I will farther relate to you the story of Saladin, and the wife of one of his vassals."

The Count begged to be allowed to hear this.

"Count," said Patronio, "Saladin was Sultan of Babylon, and being one day on an expedition with a mighty train of knights and attendants, he found it was impossible to lodge them all in the same house with himself, so he resolved to go and ask for accommodation at the residence of one of his vassals for himself, who seeing his sovereign at his humble dwelling, felt himself highly honoured thereby, and both he and his wife paid the Sultan every attention, ministering personally to all his wants. It happened that the Devil, who is ever seeking how he can tempt men to vice and folly, inspired Saladin with a violent passion for the wife of his host, and as unfortunately bad advisers, false friends, and abettors are never wanting, one of these latter counselled Saladin to send away the woman's husband on a confidential mission, pointing out that, during his absence, the wife would be in the Sultan's power. Now this advice pleased Saladin very much, so he decided on removing the husband to a distant part of his dominions. A few days after the latter's departure the Sultan returned to take up his abode at the house of his vassal, and the wife, grateful for all the benefits conferred on her house, did all in her power to please her sovereign, urging all her domestics to carefully attend to his wants.

"One day, on rising from table, Saladin passed into his own private apartments, and sent to acquaint the lady that he desired her attendance there. She, not suspecting evil, immediately went, and was both pained and surprised at hearing the Sultan declare how much he loved her. She feigned, however, not to comprehend his meaning, replying she was quite unworthy his regard, and that she daily prayed to God for his long life and happiness, as she was in duty bound, he being her lord and master, and that she never could forget his noble conduct towards her husband.

"After listening to her, Saladin replied that he loved her more than any other woman in the world. Nevertheless, she still appeared not to rightly understand his meaning, but was profuse in her professions of respect and gratitude.

"At length the Sultan was obliged to declare in plain language the nature of his passion, when the woman, who was as clever as she was virtuous, adroitly changed the conversation : ' My lord,' said she, ' I am only a poor weak woman ; still I know that men are not always masters of their feelings and passions, so it may be that you really love me as you say you do ; but this I do know, that when a man, particularly a great one like you, is influenced by a woman's charms and seeks her favour, he makes her most flattering promises, but that, as soon as he has gratified his unworthy passion, he crushes her under the weight of her own dishonour,

and basely turns his back on her; and such treatment I should richly merit were I to listen to your
declarations, which, believe me, I will neither hear
nor accept.'

"Saladin vainly endeavoured to persuade her she
had nothing to fear, as he would ever be constant
and true, protesting that, if she would but grant him
a favourable hearing, he would gratify all her wishes
and desires.

"'Well, then,' she replied, 'since you are willing
to gratify all my caprices, I promise you that as
soon as I find you are faithful to your word, I,
too, will do all you desire of me.'

"Saladin thought she was going to beg of him, as
a favour, to renounce his love for her, and hastened
to make this an exceptional circumstance from his
general promise. She reassured him, however, saying she did not require this nor any other sacrifice
beyond his strength. 'Ah, then,' cried he, 'I will
solemnly swear to do all you ask me.'

"The noble and virtuous lady, tranquillised by his
promise, knelt before him, kissing his hands and feet.
She then told him all she desired was that he should
tell her what he considered the best thing a man could
possess, and which is the head and foundation of all
other virtues, being greater in itself than all others.

"Now Saladin, hearing this question, began to
think what answer he should give, and finally asked
the good woman to grant him some time to think
the matter over; to which she consented, promising

that, as soon as he replied to her question, she would, as she had told him, comply with all his wishes. So, for the present, ended the discussion between them.

" The Sultan now sought his suite and attendants, and began questioning them, in order that he might find a suitable answer to the proposition which had been made to him.

"Some told him that, in their opinion, a life of piety and devotion and a hope centered solely on God and eternity was the greatest possession men could desire; whilst others remarked, that a life entirely given to spiritual concerns and neglectful of the duties due to our state and position could not be good. Some now proposed that loyalty was the best qualification for men; but others remarked, that a man might be very loyal, nevertheless he might be stupid, cowardly, and rude. And so they continued, each one giving some opinion; none, however, satisfying the Sultan as to the question he had proposed.

" Saladin, not finding amongst his own court any who could reply to his question, sought out two jugglers, with whom, disguised in their dress, he secretly travelled both by sea and land to seek in all countries a suitable reply to the question. They first went to the Papal court, knowing it to be the resort of Christians from all parts, hoping there to find some one able to solve their difficulty; after which they went to France, to see if, among kings, they

would succeed better.   As time passed on they
began to regret heartily the task they had under-
taken, for it appeared a man possessing discernment
enough to solve this question was not easily to be
met with, and possibly would have abandoned the
undertaking had not shame at being thought indolent
and careless prevented their so doing.   Saladin did
not think of giving up all hope, because he had not
as yet found a solution in or out of his own dominions.

" It happened that one day, as the Sultan and the
jugglers were travelling, they accidently met on the
road a young esquire who was hunting, and had
just killed a stag.   Now this young man had a very
old and feeble father who, in his younger days, was
considered the best sportsman in that country, but
now, from old age and infirmities, was confined to
his chair, still he preserved his understanding as
clear and able as when young, age having respected
his mental faculties.   The young huntsman was
coming gaily from the chase, and, meeting the Sultan
and his jugglers, he asked them who they were and
what they sought.   Hearing they were jugglers, he
invited them to accompany him home for that night.
But they excused themselves, saying they were in
great haste, it being very long since they had left
their country in search of a particular errand which
they could not complete to their satisfaction ; so that
they could not, although willing to do so, accept his
kind offer.

" Now the young man questioned them so closely

that they could not help telling him their errand, to which he replied that, in his belief, his own father was the only man on earth capable of helping them, for, if he could not answer the question, no man living could.

"When Saladin, who was disguised as a juggler, heard this he was much pleased, and they all followed the young man to his house, who entered gaily, telling his father that he had been most fortunate at the chase, and had met these men on his road home ; whereupon, explaining their difficulties, he besought his father to do his best to satisfactorily answer their question.

"The old man soon discovered that the one who interrogated him was not in reality a juggler, but acting a part. He told his son that, after they had dined, he would reply to any question they might ask him.

"The young esquire told this to Saladin, whom he believed to be a juggler, which pleased him much. As soon, however, as the tablecloth was removed after the repast, and the jugglers were ready, the old man told his son to ask them to repeat their question, assuring them that he would do his best to give a satisfactory answer, no man having yet done so.

"When Saladin, still disguised, spoke, saying that the question was, ' What is the greatest qualification a man can possess, and which is the foundation of all other virtues ? '

"The old man, hearing this, understood well its meaning, and at once recognized Saladin, having spent a long time at his court in former days and received from him many favours and marks of esteem ; he therefore said to him, 'My friend, the first answer I will give you is this, that never before to-day have jugglers been admitted to my house, and know that what I should now do would be to proclaim to all present the many favours and benefits I have received from you ; nevertheless, I will hold my peace till such time as I have had a private interview with you, not wishing to do aught which might displease you. Know, therefore, now that the greatest possession a man can own, and the source of all other virtues is *honour*, for a man will suffer death to defend his honour, it being, as it should be, his dearest treasure. For honour's sake a man refrains from doing that which he believes to be wrong, let his desire be ever so great. Hence, we see, honour is the most desirable thing a man can possess, it being the beginning and ending of all virtue and goodness, the source and crown of all. So a loss of the sense of shame is the greatest evil that can befall a man.'

" Now, when the Sultan heard these words, he understood that the old man spoke truly and justly, and, having thanked him for the explanation and also for his hospitality, prepared to depart with his companions, not, however, before the old man had informed him that, notwithstanding his disguise, he had recognized him from the first.

" Saladin, thanking his host for his polite attention, and more particularly for the solution of the question, returned with all haste to his own dominions, where, on his arrival, he was received with every demonstration of joy. After a little while he sought the residence of the lady who had proposed the question he was to reply to. She received him with every mark of respect and consideration, and insisted on his partaking of refreshments; after which Saladin related all the trouble and journeying it had cost him to have her question solved, but that, at last, he had happily succeeded in finding what he believed to be a suitable answer; and that, having thus fulfilled his promise, he hoped the lady would now keep hers made to him. To which she replied, 'Most certainly, provided the answer is satisfactory to my mind.'

"The Sultan said, 'Madam, you asked me what was the greatest treasure a man could possess, and which in itself was the author and source of all virtue and goodness. Now I answer *honour*, which is the source and foundation of all virtue.'

" The good lady, hearing this reply, rejoiced very much, and said, 'Sire, now I feel you have spoken truth to me, and have really fulfilled your promise. Now I ask you, as a king, to reply truly to the question I am going to propose; do you think there is a man in the world possessed of more honour than yourself?'

" Saladin replied that, although he felt loth to answer on his own account, still, truth obliged him

16

to say that he believed no man to be more honour-able than himself.

"The good lady, hearing this, prostrated herself at the Sultan's feet, saying, in a clear, distinct voice, ' Sire, you have told me two great truths ; first, that honour is a man's richest possession ; again, that you believe no man can be more honourable than your-self. It only now remains for you to prove the reality of your words by renouncing your intentions and relinquishing your proposals.'

"The Sultan was suddenly struck at hearing these words uttered by the lady, and immediately under-stood how she, by a happy stratagem, had saved him from committing a grievous sin and a base and dishonourable action. Thanking God, therefore, and felicitating the lady for her virtue and prudence, he assured her that he loved her more than ever, but with the truth and loyalty of a sincere and noble affection. He now recalled her husband from his distant command, and bestowed such rank, and riches, and honours on their house that their descendants now occupy the first posts in their country ; and all these happy results are due to the virtue of this noble woman, who felt in her heart, as she exem-plified in her conduct, that honour is a man's first and richest jewel, the source and foundation of all happiness.

"And as you, Count Lucanor, have requested me to inform you what is the most desirable thing for a man to possess in himself ; so I tell you it is *honour*. And be convinced that no solid virtue can exist where it is not. It makes men courageous, frank, loyal, polished in their manners, kind and charitable in their dealings with their fellow-men. It enables them to subdue their bad passions, correct irregular desires, and curb their disordered wills ; its impulses lead men to ever do that which they ought, and which is their duty, as it enables them to avoid what is wrong and unfit for them to perform. People sadly deceive themselves who imagine their ill doings are concealed because performed in secret, for every evil deed must see the light sooner or later. If we feel shame at doing wrong, how much more abashed shall we not feel at seeing our misdeeds discovered. Even a child, when about to do wrong, will depart from it, through fear of shame, without reflecting that God, who sees and knows all things, will render unto all according to their works. And now, my lord, I think I have given you a clear and definite answer to all your inquiries, and I have to thank you for the untiring attention you have kindly given to all these details. But it is certainly more than I can say for many of your suite, and especially of those who have neither the talent of attention nor the desire to understand those things which would improve them. I would compare them to those beasts laden with gold, who feel the weight which they are destined to carry, but have no knowledge of its value ; so these only feel fatigue at that which they hear, without being able to appreciate its worth or derive any benefit from it.

" And now, having replied to this, as to all your other demands, to the best of my ability, heedless of the disgust my words may have occasioned to some, I pray you to make no other requests, in order that with this example the book may be finished."

And Don Juan, holding this to be a good example, caused it to be written in this book, and composed these lines, which say as follows :—

'Tis honour chases evil from the heart ;
By honour man acts rightly without art.

NOTES.

In translating this chapter I have thought it better to use the word "honour," instead of "shame," which is really the literal meaning of the original "verguenza;" for, although honour is a word coined since Don Manuel's day, yet it is clear that it is the qualification he wished to express in his recital— that noble and generous sentiment which was the soul of chivalry, and was held next to religion by the heroes of the middle ages.

Saladin, the hero of this historical drama, has been, from his own day of the Crusades to the present time, the prototype of every valiant and chivalrous deed. His name has reappeared from century to century in prose and verse and in all languages, ever endowed with some new feature and beauty—the hero of some marvellous and heroic adventure, deeds belonging certainly more to the bright dreams of poetry than to the sober pages of recording history.

INDEX OF NAMES REFERRED TO IN COUNT LUCANOR.

www.ingramcontent.com/pod-product-compliance
Lightning Source LLC
Chambersburg PA
CBHW031343020726
47499CB00005B/1382